"Evidently ... sleeping with the boss."

Mina gazed back at him in disbelief. "How dare you—why are you treating me like this—saying such things?"

Cesare laughed softly. "That look of injured innocence, *Cara*…. I award you full marks for trying but I'm not a lonely old fool, hungry for the attention of a young, sexy woman. I'm Cesare Falcone…and if you hadn't disappeared into thin air four years ago, I'd have shredded you limb from limb for what you did to me!"

"For what *I* did to *you?*" she inquired shakily.

"But the good news is…a Sicilian never forgets being stabbed in the back, and if he has to wait a year or two…? Even better. The desire for revenge merely becomes keener."

Dear Reader,

Get ready to go back to the future with THIS TIME, FOREVER, a new series of six sweet, smart, sexy stories by our very best authors, in which men and women get a second chance for love.

Starting this month, and continuing to December, THIS TIME, FOREVER brings you a complete reunion romance every month, where passion, the past, secrets and scandals, and marriage and miracles all play their parts in bringing about the happiest of endings.

Together, forever—with Harlequin Presents!

The Editor

LYNNE GRAHAM

A Savage Betrayal

Harlequin Books

TORONTO • NEW YORK • LONDON
AMSTERDAM • PARIS • SYDNEY • HAMBURG
STOCKHOLM • ATHENS • TOKYO • MILAN
MADRID • WARSAW • BUDAPEST • AUCKLAND

For my husband, Michael—
all the romantic inspiration any woman could want.

ISBN 0-373-11824-4

A SAVAGE BETRAYAL

First North American Publication 1996.

Copyright © 1995 by Lynne Graham.

CHAPTER ONE

'AND this is my executive assistant, Mina Carroll.'

Mina shook hands and smiled as yet another introduction was made by her boss, Edwin Haland. Elegantly attired in an Armani suit, her golden hair swept up into a loose Edwardian knot, she could easily have been mistaken for a wealthy patron, rather than one of the organisers of the charity benefit. Nobody would have guessed that this was the first time she had been invited to play such a prominent role or that she was a last minute stand-in for her immediate superior, who had come down with the flu.

A hand curved round her elbow, drawing her aside. 'Where on earth did you get that suit?' Jean, their junior PR officer, hissed. 'Did you rob a bank?'

'My sister's wardrobe,' Mina whispered with dancing amethyst eyes.

'I wish we could swap sisters. Mine's into Doc Martens and vampire make-up,' Jean groaned. 'And even if I was insane enough to want to borrow something, I'd have to mug her to get it! Yours must be an angel.'

Mina laughed. 'Not quite.' She frowned at the untouched buffet and the hovering waiters. 'Why isn't the food being served?'

'Our VIP's flight has been held up.' Jean grinned. 'Of course, I forgot. You've been on holiday. You won't have met our newest sponsor yet. What a treat you have in store!'

'He must be some VIP if Mr Haland won't start without him.'

'Socially prominent, mega-rich, background of family philanthropy,' Jean told her in a mocking undertone. 'Manna from heaven. Our directors did everything but

5

kiss his feet. The more humble office mortals looked, longed and languished—even Polly, our man-hating tea lady.'

Mina's beautiful face was wreathed with amusement. 'Polly—you're joking?'

'Polly went out and bought a cream cake for him——'

'You're kidding me!'

'I'm not. He's drop-dead gorgeous. I was in the lift with him, praying it would break down...not that I expect he would have done anything with the opportunity.' Jean sighed, smoothing her hands over her ample hips. 'But you never know. Italians are supposed to like women well-stacked, and you can't say I'm not that.'

'He's Italian?' Mina had stiffened slightly.

'And there he is.'

'Where?'

'Heavens, where are your eyes?'

Mina's searching gaze shrieked to a halt on the tall, black-haired man striding down the room, flanked by two of Earth Concern's directors. Her heart gave a frantic leap behind her breastbone and every muscle pulled taut. She could feel the blood draining from her face, the sudden cold, clamminess of her flesh. She was in the grip of a shock so extreme she was paralysed by it.

'Cesare Falcone,' Jean whispered. 'Falcone Industries. Quite a coup, don't you think? Apparently, Mr Barry gave him a copy of our newsletter at some dinner and he was so impressed, he set up a meeting the same week! He even mentioned my article on waste recycling——'

'Did he?' Mina unpeeled her tongue from the roof of her dry mouth. Waste recycling? *Cesare*?

Her stomach cramping with sudden nausea, Mina turned on her heel without a word and headed for the cloakroom. Mercifully it was empty. She braced her hands on the edge of a vanity unit and slowly breathed in, struggling to combat the sick dizziness assailing her.

To see Cesare again where she had least expected to see him...when, indeed, she had *never* expected to see him again. Dear God, but life could be cruel, she thought with sudden raw bitterness.

Anger currented through her, squaring her shoulders, stiffening her spine. Four years ago, fresh out of college with a fistful of top grades, Mina had walked into what had appeared to be the plum job of her year. Cesare Falcone had hired her as his executive assistant. Three months down the line she had been sacked without warning and in the most humiliating way possible denied entrance to the Falcone building.

And, as if that had not been bad enough, she had been refused a reference. That refusal had put a big black question mark on her employment record. It had been well over a year before Mina had found another job and she had had to settle for a low-paid position without responsibility. Cesare Falcone had wrecked her career prospects in the City.

But he hadn't done it alone, she conceded with painful self-loathing. She might not have deserved the brutal treatment she had been dealt but she had played a part in her own downfall. One slip...one mistake. She had fallen in love with her employer. She had become vulnerable. Her heart had got in the way of her head. Common sense had taken a hike. And when, late one evening, Cesare had broken out the champagne over a particularly successful deal, Mina had served herself up as supper...

She closed her eyes tightly, shutting out the memories, hating them, hating herself for ever having been that naïve, that reckless, that *stupid*. If it hadn't been for that night, she would have sued for wrongful dismissal, but shame had choked her and kept her quiet when in any other circumstances she would have fought him to the last ditch for daring to terminate her contract on such terms. *Gross misconduct*. She shuddered in remembrance.

She had to drag herself back out of the cloakroom, feverishly aware that at some stage of the evening she would be forced to face Cesare. Edwin Haland was making a short opening speech by the time she returned to the crowded function-room. Everyone was already seated with their plates heaped high. Jean gave her a frantic wave from a nearby table.

Mina dropped down gratefully into the vacant seat beside the other woman. Noting her pallor, Jean frowned at her. 'You're not coming down with this flu bug, are you?'

'I'm just a bit tired.' Without appetite Mina studied the plate that Jean had helpfully filled for her.

Cesare would be seated at the top table. Mina tried hard not to look in that direction but a compulsion stronger than she was triumphed. Her heartbeat slowed to a dulled thud. 'Drop-dead gorgeous', Jean had called him and, ironically, the one time Mina hadn't noticed those sensational looks of his had been at her interview when he had stretched her with so many difficult questions that she had emerged afterwards inwardly wrung out and possessed only of the memory of dark, deep-set eyes which had seemed to be cruelly willing her to trip up and fall apart under the pressure.

After all his sardonic references to her lack of experience, she had been amazed when she had got the job. But within a week of entering employment in the Falcone building she had assumed that it was her sex which had made him put her through hoops of fire. She had discovered that she was the only female above the level of secretary on the executive floor and that the men in the boardroom unashamedly rejoiced in their chauvinism, reacting to her arrival in their midst with horror and downright resentment. Staying the course had been an uphill battle from day one...

She sank back to the present, and discovered that she was still staring, her attention roaming over his strong, dark features in profile, so familiar, even after all this time, she couldn't believe it. Her stomach clenched tight again, sudden comprehension shuddering through her to make her cringe from her own blindness.

Of course those features were familiar to her...feminised and in miniature. Hadn't she lived with those high cheekbones, those winged brows and those dark golden eyes for over three years? Her daughter, Susie, wore her parentage like a banner.

'You're nervous about the directors' meeting tomorrow,' Jean decided, finally noticing that Mina wasn't eating. 'I wouldn't worry if I were you. Your promotion's in the bag.'

Grateful to be distracted from her painful reflections, Mina sighed. 'Nothing's in the bag, Jean.'

'Mr Haland's very keen for you to head up the finance section, and the other directors will accept his recommendation,' Jean asserted in a bolstering tone.

'There were other candidates.'

'I doubt if they had your qualifications, and I would say your invitation to stand in for Simon tonight is as good as an advance announcement.'

Mina had been hoping the same thing but she didn't say so. Her self-confidence had dive-bombed in the dole queue four years ago, and her streak of bright-eyed, bushy-tailed youthful ambition had taken a similar battering. Throughout her two-week vacation, which she had spent, as she always did, at her sister's home, Mina had crossed her fingers and prayed that she would win that promotion, and not because she was eager for the higher status or the challenge of greater responsibility. No, not at all. Mina was quite simply desperate for the considerable rise in salary which would come with the position of finance manager.

Edwin was rising from the table, ushering his VIP guest to the podium. Below the lights Cesare's ebony hair had the sheen of silk, and Mina was attacked without warning by a tormentingly painful image of her own fingers sliding through those thick dark strands. Her skin burning, she dropped her head and lifted her glass of wine with an unsteady hand. Cast back in time, frantically struggling to rescue her self-discipline, she didn't absorb a single word of Cesare's speech.

But it must have been witty and amusing. Laughter broke out several times, interspersed by that appreciative silence which was the reward of a speaker talented enough to play his audience like a professional. But all she actually heard was the sound of Cesare's deep, rich voice, backed by the indolent purr of his accent. Her brain seemed incapable of taking in anything more profound.

'No wonder the directors are walking on air tonight,' Jean murmured. 'Cesare Falcone could take Earth Concern into the major leagues all on his own. Look how many journalists are here...we've never had a press turnout this good!'

People were rising from their tables and starting to mingle. Edwin signalled to Mina. With all her being she wished it were possible to ignore that gesture. She stood up, relieved to see that Cesare was being mobbed. Little wonder, she reflected cynically.

So many of their patrons only supported them because to be seen at such events lent one a certain cachet. And the chance to rub shoulders, however briefly, with Cesare Falcone, a true member of the glitterati, who when in London moved only in the most select social circles, was a chance few of their patrons would wish to miss.

'A tremendous speech, don't you think?' Edwin remarked, curving a light arm to her back, making her stiffen in surprise, as he surveyed the crush which had engulfed Cesare with unhidden satisfaction.

'Very impressive.'

'Where on earth did you get to earlier?' the older man demanded with faint irritation. 'I wanted you to sit with us at the top table.'

'I had no idea . . . sorry.' But it was a challenge to look sorry. As Mina realised what a narrow escape she had had, she felt quite light-headed with gratitude. With a little luck she would be able to slip off home soon, pull herself together and decide how she would handle being introduced to Cesare, as she surely would be sooner or later.

Tell him now, a little voice urged her. She should tell Edwin that she had once worked for Cesare, even though that fact had not appeared on her carefully doctored c.v. Edwin would be surprised, but he was highly unlikely to go back and check that same document.

'I suppose it was my fault.' He smiled, looking down at Mina, whose tiny, delicate stature never failed to remind him of his late wife. 'I should have asked you to join us.'

Picking up her courage in both hands, Mina parted her lips. 'Edwin——'

'Do you realise that this is the very first time you have called me by my Christian name?' he chuckled.

Mina flushed. She was always very formal with the directors.

'Please don't apologise,' he told her cheerfully. 'Being called Mr Haland all the time makes me feel as old as the hills.'

'Which you're far from being,' Mina said politely, a little disconcerted by the warmth she read in his eyes.

'I certainly don't feel it when I'm fortunate enough to be in the company of a very beautiful young woman. Indeed I feel privileged,' Edwin asserted with vigour, shocking her into rigidity as she glanced back up at him.

'Mr Haland?' someone intervened from behind them.

The older man's arm lifted from her narrow back with a reluctance that could be felt. Mina's cheeks were pink, embarrassment and dismay having taken hold of her. She had always been aware that Edwin Haland liked her as a quiet, hard-working member of staff, but it had not until now occurred to her that he might be attracted to her.

'Where have you been hiding yourself all evening, *cara*?'

Her downbent head flew up and then tipped back, amethyst eyes wide with apprehension, the colour highlighting her complexion evaporating fast as her gaze connected with molten gold.

'Cesare...' she whispered tautly, striving manfully to recover her composure, telling herself that she had had plenty of time to adjust to the prospect of such a confrontation but discovering to her horror that that fact seemed to make no difference to her shattered response to his sudden looming presence less than a foot from her.

'*Sì*, Cesare...who remembers you well,' he murmured in a flat undertone that chilled her, intent narrowed dark eyes scanning her pale face. 'Do I warn the old goat that he's about to fall into the alligator pit? Or do I keep my mouth shut?'

'I beg your pardon?' Mina framed without comprehension.

'From the outside it looks as though you have your sights set on a wedding-ring, but I wonder if that's true. You're a devious little bitch,' Cesare told her in a conversational tone that made what he was saying all the more shocking, 'but you're predictable. Evidently you're still sleeping with the boss.'

Totally unprepared for such an offensive attack, Mina gazed back at him in utter disbelief. 'How dare you——?'

'At the table Haland was like a dying swan in search of his mate. It didn't occur to me that it was your absence which was making him so restive, but it should have done,' Cesare told her with derision. 'There has to be some very good reason why you're working for small bucks in a charitable enterprise. Let's face it, Pollyanna you're not!'

Starting to tremble, wondering crazily if Cesare Falcone had gone mad, Mina whispered jerkily, 'Why are you treating me like this...saying such things?'

Cesare laughed softly. 'That look of injured innocence, *cara*...I award you full marks for trying but I'm not a lonely old fool, hungry for the attention of a young, sexy woman. I'm Cesare Falcone...and if you hadn't disappeared into thin air four years ago I'd have shredded you limb from limb, a piece at a time, for what you did to me!'

Unable to drag her eyes from him, Mina took an instinctive step back. She was in such shock, she couldn't even think straight. 'For what *I* did to *you*?' she repeated shakily.

'But the good news is...a Sicilian never forgets being stabbed in the back, and if he has to wait a year or two...?' Cesare spread a frighteningly expressive lean brown hand in the air between them and smiled with such chilling satisfaction that the blood in her veins ran cold. Involuntarily, she was mesmerised. 'Even better. The desire for revenge merely becomes keener, sharper...altogether more intense. I'll break you.' He closed his long fingers into his palm as if he were crushing something and laughed with wolfish amusement. 'Running was a major mistake.'

The smouldering silence thundered in her eardrums, making her feel dizzy, disorientated.

'I see you've already met Miss Carroll, Mr Falcone.' Edwin's voice intruded, making her flinch as she belatedly recalled that there were people all around them. Like a sleepwalker, suddenly woken up, Mina attempted to regain an awareness of her surroundings, but it was hopeless. Cesare's insane behaviour was already exercising her brain to full capacity.

'Mina and I require no introduction,' Cesare drawled very softly, shooting Mina's locked facial muscles a glance of veiled amusement. 'Didn't she mention our prior acquaintance?'

From somewhere, heaven knew where, Mina summoned up the self-possession to say, 'I haven't actually had the opportunity——'

'Strive for a little candour, *cara*,' Cesare cut in smoothly. 'She probably didn't mention the fact that she once worked for me because I sacked her.'

Sick to the stomach, absolutely shattered that Cesare should have calmly and smoothly dropped that shameful fact without a moment's hesitation, Mina swerved dazed eyes to Edwin. The older man's scrutiny had narrowed in astonishment and then his mouth tightened as he pressed a supportive hand to Mina's whip-taut spine. 'From the first day of her employment with us, Miss Carroll has proved herself to be an excellent, committed member of our team,' he retorted very stiffly.

'*Sì* ... Mina's ability to commit one hundred per cent is one of her most memorable qualities.' Cesare laughed suggestively half under his breath while Mina stared at him in the appalled stasis of ever-deepening incredulity. She just couldn't believe that this nightmare was really happening to her because she could not think of one single reason why Cesare should wish to humiliate her to such an extent. 'But, sadly, she is a distraction one should not risk in the office.'

Mina drew herself up to her full five feet one inch. 'If you will excuse me——'

'You're excused, *cara*,' Cesare incised in a careless aside as if she weren't there, his full attention coolly angled on Edwin Haland's efforts to conceal his outrage.

'Please excuse both of us, Mr Falcone.' The older man breathed tautly, his anger visibly warring with his uneasy awareness that Cesare was a very wealthy patron whom he had no wish to offend.

Blocking out Cesare, Mina lifted her head high, but her face was paper-white. 'I think it's time I went home.'

'I'll take you,' Edwin offered abruptly, and for some wild reason Mina felt a hysterical giggle clogging up her convulsing throat.

'That won't be necessary,' she muttered tightly, moving away a step.

'Let her back off,' Cesare suggested with the same unbelievable calm, the only one of the three of them in supreme control. 'She's in a tight corner and she doesn't want to answer awkward questions right now.'

'How dare you talk about me as if I'm not here?' Mina hissed.

'Got a little above yourself while you've been away from me, haven't you, *cara*?' Cesare glued her to the spot with an icy look of warning. 'Lose the habit fast.'

'Mr Falcone——' Edwin began.

Mina abruptly spun on her heel and walked away and it was the hardest thing she had ever had to do in her life. She reached the far side of the room, perspiration beading her upper lip, a terrible trembling quivering through her slender body in waves. Abstractedly, she registered that she was shaking with simple shock.

Had Cesare deliberately sought her out to be offensive? He had not been surprised to see her. How and why could he speak to her like that in front of her employer? Why would he set out to humiliate her in public? Why should he feel the need to smear her reputation in the most offensive possible way?

His assumption that she was sleeping with the older man had shattered her, and as for his threats... his reference to a desire for revenge... *And* he had accused her of running away four years ago! Mina prided herself on her quick intelligence but none of it made sense. The entire episode had the quality of a nightmare. The inexplicable only happened in nightmares. Why should Cesare hate her?

He *hated* her. Yes, he did. Mina lifted a slim hand to her throbbing brow but all that was travelling through her chaotic mind was, Why? Why, why, and why again? He had no reason to hate her. But Mina had every good reason to hate Cesare Falcone. Quite apart from what he had done to her career prospects, he had been the man she had loved and he had hurt her very badly. In the aftermath of that evening she had been made to feel like the cheapest, lowest of one-night stands. He had punished her for an episode in which he had played a more than equal part.

'I never mix business and pleasure, *cara*,' he had murmured that night, but she hadn't even suspected that at the same time as he was making love to her he was also planning to sack her!

Her sister, Winona, had said bluntly, '*Could* you work for him after that?' and she had known that she could not. For Cesare, that night had been a mistake and he certainly hadn't wanted her around the office after it. In one weak instant of surrender, Mina had apparently lost all claim to any form of respect or consideration.

If he had been so determined to get rid of her, he could have done so with decency. He could have offered her a transfer; Falcone Industries had branches in several other countries. Or he could at least have given her time in which to find other employment. Instead she had been ignominiously sacked on a trumped-up charge of misconduct which had blighted her prospects ever since and forced her to start again at the very bottom of the ladder.

Dear God, hadn't she suffered enough? Why did he now confront her and seek to cause her more damage? Was he off his rocker? Cesare ran a conglomerate of companies whose worth ran into multi-millions. But, insane as it might seem, maybe Cesare Falcone had a screw loose somewhere in that brilliant innovative mind...and maybe there was something peculiar about her which somehow drew out this streak of wildly illogical and destructive aggression...only how come nobody else had ever had experience of his strange behaviour?

'Do you want your coat?'

Mina blinked and found a bored-looking cloakroom attendant staring at her expectantly.

She was sliding stiff arms into her jacket when Edwin Haland appeared, looking flushed and troubled. 'Mina . . . you're leaving,' he noted awkwardly.

'It would appear to be the wisest solution,' she replied.

'I was quite appalled by his rudeness. It was inexcusable.' The older man hesitated and then pressed on in a careful undertone, 'When *did* you work for him?'

'Just after I came out of college. It only lasted three months. He did sack me.' Mina lifted her chin, her amethyst eyes strained but unflinchingly clear. 'But let me assure you that that had nothing to do with my ability as an employee. I'm afraid that the reason I was dismissed was rather more personal than that,' she completed, dry-mouthed.

Edwin looked pained, and frowned. 'It's most unfortunate. I can only hope Mr Falcone refrains from further comment in the presence of my fellow directors,' he said with grave emphasis. 'They would be most perturbed by his attitude. Mr Falcone is making a most generous contribution to our campaign, and naturally we don't want any friction between him and any member of our staff.'

Paler than ever, Mina whispered, 'I understand.'

'I'll see you tomorrow.'

His offer of a lift hadn't lasted long, not that she would have accepted it anyway. But she had noticed the determined formality he had pasted over his discomfiture. His usual rather old-fashioned friendliness had died a death in the interim since she had walked out of the room. And she wasn't at all surprised. Cesare might as well have lifted a Tannoy and called her a cheap little tramp for the benefit of the room at large.

Edwin had been shocked, had initially sought to defend her, but a few minutes' careful reflection had cooled him down and probably made him suspicious of her. After all, Cesare Falcone was a highly respected and very successful European businessman. Naturally, Edwin was now wondering what kind of behaviour it took to

provoke such a derisive attack from a man of Cesare's
education and social standing this long after the event.

A hammerbeat of tension pounded now behind her
temples. She had probably lost all chances of promotion. The position of finance manager, the successful
candidate to be announced after tomorrow's monthly
directors' meeting, would go elsewhere. Common sense
told her that Edwin had to have reservations now. How
likely was it that he would still recommend her when he
knew that Cesare Falcone despised her?

The commissionaire at the exit offered to call her a
taxi. Mina shook her head. A taxi was a luxury she
couldn't afford. She lived like a church mouse, gratefully accepted her sister's cast-off clothing, and slept in
a room no bigger than a cupboard during the week, just
existing for Friday nights when she could catch the train
back down to her sister's home in Oxfordshire. The train
fares cost her a fortune but Mina never missed a single
weekend. They were too precious. But Sunday nights
broke her heart and habit hadn't lessened the pain of
those partings from Susie. She walked down the well-lit
street, fighting not to give in to despair, but it was the
prospect of those Sunday-night partings stretching into
infinity ahead of her which she could not face.

A car purred to the kerb several yards ahead of her.
The passenger door fell open. As she hesitated, Cesare
emerged from the driver's side and stood contemplating
her over the roof of his low-slung silver Ferrari. 'Get in.
I'll give you a lift.'

'The knight of the road,' Mina framed shakily, wondering whether to scream or laugh, no longer sure what
might qualify as an appropriate response. Nothing she
had said or done had had the slightest effect on him.
He was like that truck in Steven Spielberg's first film,
Duel. She had the terrifying feeling that no matter what
she did he would keep on coming at her.

'We have unfinished business.'

Mina dropped her head, shutting out those eyes of sizzling gold which seemed to reach out and utterly intimidate. 'Leave me alone.'

'Sending me to Coventry isn't going to stop me,' Cesare murmured harshly. 'Get in the car.'

There was no hiding from the obvious. She had to find out what he meant by 'unfinished business' and straighten out whatever ludicrous misunderstanding lay behind his extraordinary behaviour. Stress had calmed her down, constrained the wilder reaches of her imagination. Cesare was ruthless, hot-tempered and as volatile as a slumbering volcano but he was *not* crazy.

She climbed in.

'I'll give you a choice,' Cesare drawled, making no attempt to start the car again.

'A choice?' she echoed blankly.

'You resign from your job.'

'Resign? Are you out of your mind?' Mina gasped in disbelief.

'If you don't resign, conscience demands that I drop a warning word in the relevant quarter,' Cesare delivered in a grim undertone. 'Finance manager—*you*? Sì...I know that you're in line for promotion. And there is no way I can stand back and let you get your greedy little paws into charitable funds.'

Mina had been sitting there staring woodenly out through the windscreen, determinedly not looking at him. Now her head spun round as though he had jerked a wire. 'Are you actually insinuating that I can't be trusted with money?' she spelt out in a strained whisper, her wide eyes incredulous at the suggestion.

'I *know* you can't be trusted.' Cesare slanted her a look of stony derision. 'Nor am I impressed by this infantile act of innocence. You committed a criminal offence four years ago and the law may not have been fast enough to pick up on the trail...but I was,' he drawled in a seething undertone, shooting her a smouldering glance of menace. 'I still have the evidence that could send you to prison——'

'*Prison*?' The single word exploded from between her dry lips, shrill and strangled, as she stared back at him in disbelief.

'Insider dealing. The courts frown heavily on the offence. You could still be tried for it.'

Every scrap of colour had drained from her cheeks. Mina tried and failed to swallow. Insider dealing. He was accusing her of having used confidential information to trade for her own benefit on the Stock Exchange. The practice was illegal.

'You're crazy...I would never have done anything like that,' Mina protested in a voice that was weak from sheer shock that he could believe her capable of such an act.

'You'd have done it more than once if I'd given you the chance,' Cesare asserted with icy bite, his profile golden and granite-hard in the street-light slanting through the windscreen. 'But I didn't. I sacked you and you took your ill-gotten gains and disappeared off the face of this planet!'

'That's not true. There weren't any ill-gotten gains because I didn't do it!' she exclaimed shrilly, her heart pounding madly with fright against her ribcage.

Cesare's ice-cold stare told her just how unimpressed he was by her protests.

'I thought you sacked me because—because I slept with you!' She had to force out the statement and she couldn't bring herself to look at him.

'*Dio mio*! The jury will surely break down and cry when they hear that defence,' Cesare said with flat derision. 'It is on record that you were sacked for gross misconduct.'

'I know, but I——'

'Popular report suggests that some prisons harbour big butch women. At seven stone and built like a doll, maybe you should consider getting into training.'

Mina was in such turmoil that she shrank back against the passenger door in horror. 'I'm not going to prison...I haven't done anything!'

'Well, you're certainly not about to do anything in the charity world.' Cesare shot the assurance at her with cold threat. 'With your talent for accounting, you could work any number of scams. I want you out of there as of now——'

'But I haven't done anything...I'm not dishonest!' Mina slung back at him in helpless repetition and growing apprehension.

'If you push me I'll tell Haland, and I can back my allegations up with cold, hard evidence,' Cesare returned with slashing cool. 'And a man like Haland, with all those fine, upstanding principles, might just feel that when he's informed of an illegal act it is his duty to report it to the authorities——'

'And if you were so convinced I was guilty, why didn't you call them in?' Mina demanded wildly, fighting to find some angle on which she could base a defence.

'It would have been like reporting a murder without the corpse. You'd vanished like a thief in the night.' Cesare lounged back with indolent relaxation and surveyed her intently, eyes slivers of molten gold beneath the luxuriant fringe of his ebony lashes. 'And I did entertain myself briefly with a vision of you becoming a prison mascot, but ultimately it didn't satisfy me. I think the punishment should fit the crime——'

'I haven't committed any crime...why won't you listen to me?' she gasped.

'You used pillow-talk for profit——'

'*Pillow-talk*?'

'You ripped off that information like a professional. You made a fool of me. I could have been dragged down in the dirt with you. Guilty by association. I have no doubt you intended to say that you traded on my behalf if you were caught,' Cesare told her very softly, every accented syllable dropping into the throbbing silence.

'Pull the dumb dizzy blonde act and insist you had no idea that what you were doing was against the law.'

'You're out of your m-mind!' Mina was white, barely able to vocalise.

'Say you were seduced, *used*,' Cesare continued with harshened emphasis, pinning her to the spot with smouldering dark golden eyes that burned. 'If you were a man I'd have killed you...but you're a woman and I intend to use you exactly as you used me...'

CHAPTER TWO

'I BEG your pardon?' Mina was still reeling with shock, her brain thrown into total chaos by the shattering accusation that Cesare Falcone had dropped on her four years after the event.

There was too much for her to take in all at once. But, devastated though she was, there had been a terrifying ring of reality to his derision when she had tried to protest her belief that she had been fired for the sin of once sharing his bed. No matter how insane his allegations, she suddenly had no doubt that he truly believed that she had committed a crime. It explained his attitude towards her. Both in the present and in the past. His hatred and his aggression now made sense out of what had earlier seemed like insanity.

Her mind was working in slow motion, one tiny step at a time. Cesare thought she had been guilty of insider dealing. Worse, he believed she had used information which he had given her in trust. Worse still, he was convinced that if she had been apprehended by the authorities she would have lied and said she had been acting on his behalf and not her own.

'I shall use you as you once set out to use me,' Cesare asserted.

She cleared her throat with difficulty. 'And how are you planning to do that?'

'How do you think?' Cesare dealt her a look of grim amusement. 'I don't think you'll ever tangle with a Sicilian again.'

Mina drew in a deep, shaky breath. 'I intend to take legal advice about the allegations you have made against me.'

'Cast-iron allegations with proof.'

'You couldn't possibly have proof of something I didn't do!'

'If you've got any of that money left, I intend to take it off you. By the time I am finished with you——'

'You're not even going to *start* with me!' Mina told him, suddenly frantic to get out of the Ferrari but wanting to do so with dignity.

A hard smile slashed Cesare's expressive mouth. 'Don't tell me I can't do what I've already begun. Did you really think that I would let you get away with it? You should have known I would be on your trail. It made my day when I saw your photo——'

'My photo?'

'On the front of Earth Concern's newsletter. That was a careless move, but then you were unlucky. My staff deal with the charity flyers. Rarely have I had such literature thrust at me at dinner parties,' Cesare said very drily. 'But there you were, looking all prim and proper, standing beside Haland at some fund-raiser.'

Mina had forgotten that she had featured in that same newsletter which Jean had mentioned as having ignited Cesare's interest in the charity. She had assumed that their meeting tonight had been a ghastly coincidence and that he had not realised that she worked for Earth Concern until he'd seen her. The news that he had had that prior knowledge shook her.

'A lying, conniving little confidence trickster like you working in a position of trust for a charitable concern,' Cesare outlined softly. 'A concern no doubt full of well-intentioned people, motivated more by environmental awareness than good business sense and strict control of their funds. And along comes Mina like a fox into a coop of little fluffy chicks waiting to be plucked. Haland's blood would freeze in his veins if he knew what you were capable of!'

'How dare you call me a confidence trickster?' Mina objected strickenly, her breath rasping in her throat. 'There has been some hideous misunderstanding——'

'And it would appear to be on your side.' Cesare treated her to a look from hooded golden eyes that was curiously chilling. 'I've tracked you down and I know exactly what you are. Don't preach to the converted. Watching you simper up at Haland and blush took me way back. And you're so cute, you're so *little*,' he stressed, studying her slight figure with blistering derision, his mouth twisting and then compressing into a bloodless line. 'You make men feel protective. You stitched me up, too. I don't blame the old goat for falling for the fragile feminine act hook, line and sinker. *Dio mio*, didn't I fall for it too?'

The atmosphere was explosive. Suppressed rage quivered through every syllable in that final statement. Anger so fierce that she could taste it vibrated in him. Her mouth was dry, 'Cesare, I——'

He reached out a powerful hand, closed it round one slender wrist and yanked her bodily forward. 'Shut up,' he intoned with vicious bite. 'I won't ever fall for it again, *cara*. I know how clever you are, but your greed betrays you as surely as a streak of fundamental stupidity. You're a treacherous bitch, but life as you know it is about to change. Betraying me was a big mistake.'

Trembling, trapped by his immensely greater strength, she gaped at him. 'I didn't betray you!'

'You betrayed me in every way there was. As an employee and as a lover!' Cesare raked at her. 'One unforgettable night when my every fantasy was fulfilled. A virgin, but a whore in the making!'

Mina lifted her free hand and hit him a crack across one hard cheekbone that numbed her fingers. And then she froze, appalled by the violence that had roared up inside her from a place she didn't know. She had never struck another human being before.

'Relax . . . you were the best I ever had.'

Mina went white, her lower lip wobbling. Cesare hadn't even flinched from that ringing slap. Disorientatingly, he smiled, and that smile chilled her to her bones. It was like the smile on the face of a tiger after drawing first blood. He knew she had lost control and he was triumphant, even amused. With a soft laugh, he released her wrist.

Her breath sobbed in her throat as she made a frantic attempt to get out of the car, but the door wouldn't open.

'It's locked,' Cesare said gently, and fired the engine.

'Where are you taking me?'

'Back to your pathetically poor bed-sit. Presumably chosen to yank at Haland's heart-strings. He must be very naïve,' Cesare delivered. 'Ain't no way what you've got on your back fits the poverty-stricken image you're striving to put out for his benefit.'

'The suit is borrowed,' Mina said jerkily, and she didn't even know why she was bothering to make that trivial explanation. Her nerves felt like elastic cruelly stretched and ready to snap.

'Sure it is,' Cesare mocked. 'Fits like a glove, too. You just happen to have a best friend as short as you are?'

Mina pressed an unsteady hand against her throbbing temples. 'How do you know where I live?'

'I know.'

'Please let me out of this car.'

'So that you can scarper? One false move in that direction, *cara*, and you'll live to regret it for the rest of your life.'

'Stop threatening me!'

'Beginning to feel those claustrophobic prison walls closing in around you, *cara*?' he chided.

'Since there is not the remotest chance that I could be in danger of going to prison for something I *haven't* done,' Mina stressed in the sudden fury that finally broke through layer after layer of shock, 'I'm not too bothered!'

'Liar...you're shaking in your child-sized shoes. But it ought to be a relief to escape the shackles of the clean-living, do-gooding role you've been playing for Haland's delectation. Not that you appeared to enjoy having your image dented this evening,' Cesare reminded her without remorse.

'What you said was unforgivable!'

'I told the whole truth and nothing but the truth. I was tempted to tell him a whole lot more but I would have looked tacky then,' he conceded wryly.

'I am not resigning from my job.'

'Then I bring the roof down on you. I withhold my donation to Earth Concern's excellent work in the field of environmental awareness——'

'You wouldn't!' Mina exclaimed in horror.

'And I explain that I cannot place such a large sum of money in the control of a charity employing a woman I know to be untrustworthy and dishonest.'

Mina bent her head, utterly shattered by the speed of that unflinching assurance.

'I should think you would be as welcome at the office as a blizzard in July after that.'

'I could sue you for defamation of character!' Mina threw at him wildly.

'And the evidence I would produce would throw the case out of court on the first day and leave you facing other, even less palatable options. I'd nail you to the wall—why risk marking that beautiful skin?'

He could not have evidence of something she hadn't done! But evidently someone in Falcone Industries, someone at board level *had* been insider dealing. Cesare had found evidence and mistakenly traced it back to her. Was that some horrible accident or was it possible that the real guilty party had deliberately laid a false trail which implicated her? Was she being paranoid? Her flesh chilled at the idea that four years ago somebody she worked with might well have set her up as a target to protect his own back.

In the thundering silence Cesare pulled the Ferrari into the kerb and killed the engine. 'Where do you go at weekends?' he murmured lazily.

Mina went rigid, her golden head spinning round, stricken amethyst eyes wide before she hurriedly veiled them.

Cesare lounged back in his seat, his vibrantly handsome features hard as marble in the shadows. 'Every weekend...every vacation,' he spelt out, toying with her by revealing how much he already knew about her movements. 'Do you have a husband tucked away somewhere—a partner in crime?'

'Don't be r-ridiculous!'

'A lover, then,' Cesare decided with complete impassivity. 'He's out. I won't be giving you weekends off——'

'What on earth are you talking about?'

'Or the freedom to sneak into other beds. Though I doubt that you'll have the energy. You'll be fully occupied keeping me happy, and I'm not that easy to live with round the clock,' Cesare mused, quite untouched by the stunned look on her face. 'I'm low on patience, high on demand——'

'I'm not going to be living with you,' Mina mumbled in a choked voice.

'I don't care what you call it, but you are most certainly going to be the leading feature in my bed every night.' Cesare rested his ebony head back with indolent grace and appraised her with eyes that glittered diamond-hard, his relaxation emphasising his innate confidence that he had the whip-hand.

'You're off your trolley!' Mina snatched in a jagged breath, outrage taking over. 'I'd throw myself off a cliff before I'd let you touch me again!'

'I don't think so...'

'I know so!' Mina launched back.

'You got something else to trade for my silence?' Cesare enquired smoothly as he slanted a sardonic smile at her.

As the ramifications of that question sank in, Mina's shattered gaze clung to his cool gold one. 'You're trying to blackmail me,' she whispered in horror.

'Has to be the knock-on effect of the low company I'm keeping.' Cesare cast her an intent look, unconcerned by her accusation. 'And it's not one quarter as sordid as what you did to me. You traded sex for information and profit. You sold me out for the requisite thirty pieces of silver. What does that make you? You used me——'

'I wouldn't use anyone like that!'

'Pay-back time, *cara*. Don't bother working out your notice for Haland. That's over and he'll never know what a narrow escape he had, thanks to my intervention. I'll pick you up tomorrow night at eight. OK,' he positively purred, and it wasn't a question. 'You can go and get your beauty sleep now.'

Mina swallowed hard and began to slide out of the car, but Cesare moved too and reached for her before she could register what he intended. He tugged her back across the seat as if she were a doll. 'Come here...'

'Get your hands off me!' she exploded.

'I want something on account first.'

Anchoring long fingers into her silky hair, Cesare held her fast, sweeping her upturned face with heavily lidded golden eyes.

'Let...go...of...me,' Mina told him breathlessly.

'Take up the weight training—you're likely to be in dire need of it.' His accented drawl had thickened and fractured, spilling out warning flares into an atmosphere already vibrating with fierce tension.

'No...' she mumbled, clashing unavoidably with the scorching charge of his heated gaze.

'Never say no to me,' Cesare intoned huskily. 'When you slam a door in my face, I kick it down.'

She had forgotten—oh, dear God, how could she have forgotten?—how he could make her feel. It was terrifying... It was as though a physical force-field en-

closed her, locking out every brain-wave. Her own
heartbeat pounded in her eardrums. Excitement, raw and
dangerous, leapt through every single skin-cell. Her
breasts were already stirring beneath the thin barrier of
her bra, her nipples pinching into sudden painful
tightness.

'Stop it...' she framed unevenly, yet she was trapped
in unmoving stasis.

'But I'm not doing anything...*yet*.' He lowered his
gleaming dark head slowly. Her breath hung suspended
and then he pressed his mouth hotly to the tiny pulse
flickering wildly above her collarbone. Every bone in
her body melted in a burst of feverish heat. Her head
fell back, her throat extending. She trembled violently,
an upswell of sensation suddenly released with devastating force. Her hands flew up of their own volition,
one finding his shoulder, the other spearing into his hair,
and just touching him again felt so good that she ached.

Raising his head, he ravaged her soft mouth with a
sudden devouring hunger that took her by storm. He
prised her lips apart with the tip of his tongue and then
plundered the tender interior with carnal expertise. Her
fingernails dug into his shoulder, a passion wilder than
anything she had ever known consuming her as she
answered that sensual demand, returning his kisses with
all the fire of her own response.

Without warning, Cesare tore himself free. Hard hands
clamping round her slender forearms, he thrust her back
from him, fierce derision stamped in his lean features
as he looked down at her and released his pent-up breath
in a hiss. 'Natural talent like you wouldn't believe,' he
drawled with contempt. 'Maybe I picked the wrong punishment... or maybe you're stupid enough to think you
can con me into leaving you cosily ensconced in that
charity.'

Mina wiped the back of her hand across her reddened
mouth in a violent gesture of shuddering self-disgust.
Her amethyst eyes shimmered with hatred. Wrenching

at the door, she shot out of the car and stood on the pavement, ashamed to discover that her legs felt weak and shaky.

'If you don't leave me alone, you'll find that you're digging up a whole lot more trouble than you'll want to handle!' she told him tightly.

'Is that a threat?' Cesare enquired softly.

Mina wanted to scream. Briefly she closed her burning eyes. 'No, Cesare, that's not a threat, because, unlike you, I don't make threats. It's a warning. You wrecked my life four years ago and only now do I find out why...' As her throat closed over, her voice cracked and she threw her head back, snatching in oxygen to continue. 'But whoever it was who traded information for profit it wasn't me! You've got the wrong culprit——'

'Like hell I have!'

'I won't allow you to victimise me again,' Mina swore tremulously, a tide of dammed-up tears gritty behind her eyelids. 'I need my job and I'm not resigning from it! So leave me alone!'

'Tomorrow night—eight,' Cesare specified, and slammed the door.

Minutes later, Mina sank down on her bed in her tiny room and covered her working face with her hands. Insider dealing—how could he have believed that of her? How many twenty-two-year-olds fresh out of college would be up to such illegality? Where was she supposed to have got the funds which would have been necessary even to begin playing the stock market? Four long years, and she was only finding out now that that was why he had sacked her!

He had accused her of disappearing into thin air. That meant that he must have tried to contact her again. She loosed an embittered laugh. She had received the notice of her termination of employment outside working hours. It had been delivered by special messenger and it had come all the way from Hong Kong, where Cesare had been at the time.

She had been within days of moving into a new flat, but the loss of her job had meant that she could no longer afford to make that move. It had also meant that she had to surrender the sizeable deposit she had put down. If Roger and Winona had not returned from France because her brother-in-law's father was seriously ill, she might well have found herself homeless. Only three months out of college, her financial situation had been anything but buoyant.

But not too many weeks had gone by before Mina was forced to face the fact that her wrecked career, her broken heart and her savaged sense of humiliation could be completely overshadowed by the hard reality of an unplanned pregnancy. Cesare's child, conceived in love, passion and irresponsibility. Mina had been devastated by the discovery that she was expecting a baby. After a great deal of heartache and soul-searching, she had reached the painful conclusion that the best option for her unborn child was adoption.

'We'll see,' Winona had said quietly. And when her baby was born Mina had found that she could not bear to part with her, and the past three years had been one long, tough struggle to give her daughter the best she could, and for over two years that had meant living apart from Susie during the week and seeing her only at weekends.

Dear God, she hated Cesare, and yet when he had hauled her into his arms, when he had kissed her... Furiously she scrubbed at her swollen mouth again, loathing herself. How could he make her feel like that again? Her response had been mindless, wanton and utterly divorced from intellect. Four years ago she had been head over heels in love, and the passionate desire he had awakened in her had for the whole of one unforgettable night seemed as natural a part of that love as breathing.

But the events which had followed had taught her to bitterly regret her own lack of control. She could not even say that Cesare had misled her as to the exact nature of his intentions. They had gone in the space of minutes from the first kiss to the nearest bed, and she hadn't once thought about what she was doing—indeed, had fondly imagined that Cesare had been similarly swept away by an explosive passion.

Now a little older, and she hoped a lot wiser, she knew differently. Cesare had simply taken what he realised was on offer and she had been pitifully naïve, the victim of her own equally silly romantic fantasies, to think for one moment that it meant anything more to him than the slaking of a momentary lust for a female body.

And tonight he had reached for her in a macho power-play, seeking to humble her even further. Instead of angrily fighting him off, she had welcomed him, unable to resist the raw potency of his attraction. The acknowledgement filled her with shame. Was it any wonder that Cesare fondly imagined she was promiscuous? Maybe that was preferable to him thinking that she was sex-starved and a push-over, she decided, inwardly cringing from the painful revelation of her own weakness.

On a rolling wave of angry defiance, she got into bed. Tomorrow she was going into work. She would call his bluff. Tonight Cesare had had the advantage of surprise, and she had been so shocked by his accusations that he had walked all over her. But if he showed up tomorrow night she would call the police and accuse him of harassing her! See how he liked that...

Who the heck did he think he was? Not content with falsely accusing her of a crime, he then tried to deny her the right to earn a living, and he threatened her! Then, she knew Cesare's temperament. Cesare was a creature of deep, dark moods where his emotions were concerned, and Cesare had been seething for the past four years.

It was funny how that made her feel good—the thought of him seething quite took her headache away. Susie had that temper too, she reflected, and then pushed the too intimate acknowledgement away again. Suddenly she began looking at the situation from his point of view, and on some insanely illogical level his view—briefly—tickled her pink.

Cesare believed she had run rings round him. He might be all smooth sophistication on the surface, but underneath he was as liberated as Stone Age man. The mere idea that a woman had put one over on him must have been a deeply devastating blow to his ego. A concept so injurious to his pride was an insult to his masculinity. Therefore the slur had to be wiped out, the balance redressed...but in private. Well, if Cesare thought for one slippery moment that she was dumb enough to be blackmailed back into his bed, it was time he thought again!

Mina was on the phone at about eleven o'clock when Edwin Haland made his first appearance the next morning. He looked tired and strained and he avoided her gaze as he passed by her desk and entered his office. A few minutes later, he called her in.

He cleared his throat awkwardly. 'I'm late in because I had an appointment at Falcone Industries.'

Mina tensed, her brows drawing together.

'After what I witnessed last night, I felt I had to enquire further into the reasons for your dismissal.'

She turned very pale, her spine tautening. 'I gather you weren't satisfied with my explanation——'

'It wasn't a question of personal feelings,' he said heavily. 'But I was troubled that you had concealed the fact that you had formerly been employed by Cesare Falcone.'

Mina stiffened and flushed but she made no comment. An honest c.v. wouldn't have got her a job with Earth Concern and she had been desperate to find employment at the time.

'There's no point in dragging this sorry business out.' Edwin Haland sighed with unhidden discomfiture. 'I'm afraid that dishonesty with money is not a matter which can be overlooked in an enterprise such as this.'

In a daze of sick shock, Mina flinched. Cesare had brought the roof down on her exactly as he had threatened to do, yet for some ridiculous reason she did not want to accept that even Cesare could expose her to this level of appalling humiliation. 'But I——'

Edwin moved a silencing hand. 'I really don't want the details, Mina.'

'Have you ever heard of innocent until proven guilty?' Mina probed shakily.

He turned his head away and made no response. 'I would like to ask you to tender your resignation without dragging us all through a great deal of unpleasantness. During your time with us you have been an excellent worker, and I am willing to give you a reference on the basis of those two years.'

'You want me to leave because Cesare doesn't want me here and you're scared he'll withhold the funds he's promised for the campaign,' Mina translated between clenched teeth. Woodenly, she nodded. 'Fine. I'll leave now. But when I clear my name, Edwin, you will apologise to me, because I believed that you, at least, knew me better than this!'

Never mind the promotion you were worrying about, what about the job you thought you did have? she thought as she left his office. In the space of twenty-four hours, Cesare had shattered her life again. And she couldn't believe it. Of course, she could have stayed on at the charity until they found a real reason to sack her, but her pride was too great to stand the mortification of working beside a man who thought she was some kind of a thief and who could no longer meet her eyes! As it was she had a reference and Edwin's assurance that he would not tell anyone why she had chosen to leave.

Everything up in smoke! Acrid tears burned her eyes. How long would it take her to find another job? How long to prove herself again? Her plans to bring Susie up to London to live with her as soon as she could afford somewhere better to live had been blown to smithereens, and she had worked so long towards that goal.

Now, all of a sudden, she was back where she had been three years ago but far less optimistic. Dear heaven, why had she ever got involved with Cesare Falcone? He was like a curse following her around. What had she ever done to deserve this? Awash with rage and humiliation, Mina's sense of injustice was bitterly intense, but beneath all of that was this terrible pain that Cesare could have sunk so low.

She was walking down the street where she lived when she saw the Ferrari. Ferraris were not a regular sight there. The glossy paintwork gleamed in the sunshine, a jewel in a sea of beat-up cars. She knew it was Cesare. When she was within twenty feet, he sprang out and strode round the bonnet.

She stopped dead, smitten with bloodlust at the sight of him, finding every single detail of his immaculate appearance offensive: the light grey Italian suit, tailored to a perfect fit over those wide shoulders and long, lean legs, the pale blue silk shirt which accentuated the all-the-year-round gold of his skin, the hand-stitched shoes. A couple of giggling teenage girls on the other side of the street wolf-whistled at him. Par for the course for Cesare. He was a visual feast, she conceded with a spasm of self-hatred.

'Mina...'

'Come to gloat?' she slashed back at him, wondering why he wasn't smiling like the shark he was. In fact, as he stilled in the sunlight, she noticed his tension. It sprang out at her in the tautness of stance, his clenched jawline, the darkness of his deep-set eyes below his level brows.

'It wasn't me who spoke to Haland. I was out of the office,' he intoned flatly.

Why did that sound so much like a plea for understanding? What a crazy idea, she thought, consigning it to oblivion. Cesare knew how to do an awful lot of things, but pleading didn't feature in the list. And what did he mean by saying that *he* hadn't spoken to her former employer?

'He saw Sandro,' Cesare completed.

Cesare's brother, Sandro the creep, Mina reflected with an inner shudder of distaste. Her stomach heaved at the awareness that Sandro was apparently acquainted with the murky details of her so-called dishonesty.

A mere year Cesare's junior, Sandro was a foul-mouthed, workshy, ignorant boor who without the protection of his big brother would not have been employed by any reputable company. That Sandro had been in a position to destroy her reputation in a cosy little chat with Edwin Haland was somehow the most gross betrayal of all. It was the ultimate humiliation.

'It doesn't really matter who saw him, does it? Unless you're back-tracking on what you said last night and were planning to mount a cover-up on my behalf!' Mina vented a sharp little laugh at that ridiculous idea and surveyed him with unhidden loathing.

Cesare was oddly pale beneath his bronzed skin. His gaze flared gold as he connected with that look of hers, and his beautifully shaped mouth twisted. Mina stood there, quivering with bitter resentment and distress, and damned him with her eyes.

'We need to talk,' he murmured in a taut undertone.

'The only person I need to talk to right now is a solicitor, and I am so grateful that your slime-bag of a brother has put himself in the hot seat beside you, because now I can kill two birds with one stone...and, believe me, I intend to!' Mina slung at him rawly, yet knowing even as she spoke that there was no way she would carry out such a threat. 'Now get out of my way!'

His strong jawline clenched. 'I would not advise approaching a solicitor——'

'Oh, boy, I just bet you wouldn't! After all, it's a free world, isn't it? It's OK for you to go around telling filthy lies about me and putting me out of yet another job, but no, it wouldn't be a good idea for me to try and defend myself. Who do you think you're kidding?' Mina demanded aggressively, her fists clenching when he still neglected to step out of her path. '*Move*, Cesare!'

Cesare continued to stare at her as though he was mesmerised, brooding golden eyes intently fixed on her. Outraged by his lack of response, Mina planted a small hand against his broad chest to thrust him out of her way. A lean hand whipped up and unexpectedly trapped hers, preventing her from withdrawal.

'What the heck are you——?' she began.

Without the smallest warning he grabbed her right there in the middle of the street. Two strong hands clamped to her waist as he lifted her up against him and brought his mouth smashing down on hers with an explosive sexual hunger that travelled through her like forked lightning.

A stifled gasp of shock escaped low in her throat and then, equally abruptly, Cesare was lowering her back to the pavement again, sliding her with instinctive sensuality against every fiercely taut line of his long, powerful body.

Her head swimming, her mouth tingling, every thought an effort, she discovered for herself what had provoked that sudden assault. Her cheeks burned as she felt the unmistakable thrust of his male arousal. In the middle of an argument, too, she conceded, hopelessly disconcerted by the mysteries of the masculine libido.

'*Dio*!' he grated in a seething undertone. 'I want you so much, I *ache* . . .'

CHAPTER THREE

SUDDENLY appalled by the awareness that she was standing submissively in the circle of his arms, Mina broke free, clumsily side-stepped him and vanished through the battered door a few feet behind him. She thudded up the narrow stairs, reaching the top landing in record time as she fumbled for her key and stuck it in the lock. She only heard Cesare behind her as she pushed open the door.

'Go away!'

In one long stride he was in front of her, preventing her from slamming the door in his face. '*Per amor di Dio...*' he whispered, looking over the top of her head at the tiny, claustrophobic room as bare and tidy as a cell.

'I don't want you in here!' Mina snapped.

With an arrogant hand, Cesare pressed her back and stepped inside. There was very little floor space. There was a bed, a small table against one wall to carry a two-ring burner, and a curtained alcove for storage on the other. He surveyed his surroundings with an air of incredulous distaste.

'It's clean. You're not likely to catch anything.' Mina was horribly embarrassed but struggling not to show the fact. 'Maybe you'd like to conduct a search for the loot you're so convinced I've got!'

Cesare angled his dark head back to her. 'You cleared over a quarter of a million pounds on the stock-market. I assume you have it salted away somewhere safe—perhaps in property down in the country where you spend your weekends?' Diamond-hard dark eyes glittered over her, scanning for the smallest change of expression.

39

Her lower lip dropped from her upper. 'A quarter of a million, and you think I'd be living here like a rat in a cage?'

'It would have been very foolish of you to flaunt it, but *this* . . .' Cesare spread fastidious brown fingers as he took another almost fascinated glance around. 'This dump is decided overkill. Your salary at Earth Concern might have been low, but it would certainly have enabled you to live more comfortably than this,' he informed her drily.

'Maybe I have expenses you don't know about.' As soon as she said it she regretted it, her profile pinching tight with tension. 'A quarter of a million,' she muttered in a hurried aside, very tempted to laugh like a hyena as she imagined how different the last few years would have been had she had access to even a tithe of that amount of money.

'What did you do with it?' Cesare enquired grimly.

'I never had it, for goodness' sake,' Mina retorted wearily, suddenly totally fed up with the thankless task of reiterating her innocence to someone determined not to listen to her.

'You deposited fifty thousand in your current account—what did you do with the rest of it?'

Fifty thousand. Alarm bells went off like Klaxons inside her head. A month after Mina had been sacked she had been stunned to receive a bank statement which informed her that she was miraculously fifty thousand pounds richer than she had thought she was. She had immediately contacted the bank to tell them that there had been a mistake and that the money they had credited to her àccount could not be hers. Incredibly they hadn't been interested and had indeed assured her that there had been no mistake.

For a couple of days she had actually wondered if Cesare had deposited the money as a pay-off to salve his own conscience for the brutal way he had treated her. But that explanation had struck her as unlikely. In all, it had taken her quite a few weeks to persuade the bank that they had to take that money back out of her account. Finally they had done so and a while after that, when she had asked, a bank clerk had gone off to enquire and returned to tell her that yes, there had been a mistake and the money had since been returned to its true owner.

'How did you know what was in my account?' Mina probed.

'I have my methods. Now perhaps you'll cease this painful refusal to admit the truth,' Cesare suggested.

Mina burned with bitterness. It was too much of a coincidence. She *had* been smoothly set up as a fall guy. Cesare had been able to trace some of the money right back to her. Somebody had laid a careful trail for him, but who? And how could she ever find out and prove her own innocence? Surely the bank had a record of that transfer of the fifty thousand into another account? Well, she wasn't about to waste her breath sharing her suspicions with Cesare, who would doubtless think that in fear of investigation *she* had transferred the money elsewhere in a belated attempt to cover her own tracks.

'You've only been with that charity for two years,' Cesare persisted. 'Where were you for the other two years? Travelling? Partying?'

It had been no blasted party in that labour ward, Mina thought in sudden rage; nor had the second year been any more entertaining. Ignoring family protests, she had been determined to go it alone with Susie. She had worked in a series of lousy jobs, most often brought to an end by an inability to find a reliable child-minder whom she could afford to pay.

In fact she had practically starved before she'd accepted that she could either fall back on the social services, who would then have sought child support for Susie from Cesare, or go back to Roger and Winona with her tail between her legs. Of the two options, family had won out. Mina would sooner have slept on a park bench than have Cesare know that she had given birth to his child. A man who slept with you one night and sacked you the next was hardly keen father material. Cesare had made his indifference cruelly clear. He had treated her like the dirt beneath his feet and she would never, ever forget that experience.

'Partying,' Cesare decided, searching her flushed and defensive face.

Mina threw back her head, provoked beyond tolerance. 'Why not?'

'Who with?' Cesare grated roughly.

Mina shrugged, moving a few feet to the small window, bitterly amused by his anger. Fool that she was, she hadn't seen this weakness in Cesare last night. He still wanted her; he still found her attractive. Why was she so shattered by that revelation? Sexual chemistry did not automatically go hand in glove with respect and liking. Hadn't she learnt that to her own cost last night? She hated him but he could still smash her defences just by touching her, just by coming too close, awakening her with the flaring gold of his beautiful eyes. Cesare was a very sexual personality. So why shouldn't he be vulnerable too? It was poetic justice.

'I asked you who with?' he repeated curtly.

'Far be it from me to ask what business that is of yours!' Mina spun round and her eyes clashed with the glittering gold threat in his.

'I want to know, and I also want to know where you go at weekends,' he spelt out between clenched teeth.

'Do I get to ask what you've been doing with your weekends for the past four years?' Mina suddenly heard herself spit back at him, and she didn't even know where that question had come from, didn't recall thinking it. But all of a sudden she knew she hated Cesare even more than she had thought.

'I asked you first. How many men have you been with?'

'How many women have you been with?' she launched back furiously.

Cesare snatched in an audible breath and strode forward. 'The weekends. Who is he?'

Mina reflected on the considerable amount of time she spent with Roger's grandfather, whom she had known since she was three years old. Baxter Keating was a lovely old man, who shared his large country house with Roger and Winona and was as careful as Mina was not to intrude any more than necessary on the couple's privacy.

'He's a lot older than you,' she murmured with vicious sweetness, wanting to shock, wanting to anger.

Cesare went rigid, satisfyingly so. 'Married?'

'Widowed.'

'Is he likely to marry you?' he bit out.

'No,' she said with perfect truth.

'But you go down to his home at weekends...and you live with him,' Cesare framed in a thunderous, raw undertone that sent tiny little tremors running up her taut spinal column. A confession that she spent her weekends at orgies could not have drawn a more appalled response.

'If you didn't want the truth, you shouldn't have asked,' Mina dared, priding herself on not having told a single lie. And, since what she had pretended to confess would naturally be a total turn-off for a man as fastidious as Cesare, hopefully he would now leave her alone.

With a nerve-racking abruptness that made her flinch, he swung away from her and then disconcertingly swung back, his strong face set like stone. 'Presumably he bought the clothes you were wearing last night?'

'Yes.' Roger worked for his grandfather, managing the family estate. Roger financed Winona's wardrobe.

'Clearly you have spent all the money.'

'I have a small overdraft.' Gosh, this dialogue was fun, she thought nastily, enjoying the feeling that she had Cesare on the run.

His eloquent mouth was flattened into a bloodless line but there was an arc of darker colour highlighting his savage cheekbones and the stark clarity of his gaze. 'Without shame, you admit to me that you are——'

'Morally weak.'

'The activities you confess to are not one step removed from prostitution,' Cesare condemned with the oddest tremor interfering with his usually perfect diction.

Mina lost colour but held fast. He was absolutely disgusted. Another few minutes and he would be gone, put to flight by her moral depravity.

'Haland?' he enunciated.

Mina reddened fiercely. 'No!'

'*Madre di Dio* ... God has some mercy...' Cesare expelled his breath and surveyed her with fiercely narrowed eyes. 'You will not communicate in any way with this man again,' he told her with menacing harshness. 'Nor will you ever offend me again by referring to the liaison.'

Events had taken a sudden violently off-balancing swerve into unknown and unexpected territory. Mina blinked rapidly. 'I——'

'Not another word,' Cesare cut in rawly. '*Dio*! How the hell could you tell me such truth? Could you not have lied?' He spat something in angry Italian, slashed a furious hand through the air, making her jump back a step, and then appeared to get a grip on his rage again. 'No, it is better that I know the truth.'

'I think you should go now.' Mina was keen to give him a helping hand back in the direction of the exit she had been expecting him to make.

'Why?' Cesare slung her a derisive look of smouldering aggression. 'When you've just given me the price——'

Without understanding, she frowned. 'What price?'

'You're the one who has told me that you are any man's possession for the right price, and I'm prepared to pay it to have you in my bed,' Cesare drawled with a positive shudder of unconcealed fury.

Sharply disconcerted by the even less anticipated response he was now making, Mina licked her dry lips. 'I——'

'You told me quite deliberately, you shameless...' With a seething hiss, Cesare clenched his oven white teeth and bit back whatever he had been about to call her. 'You *know* how much I want you. You just stuck on a price-tag!'

Mina almost choked in an effort to swallow. Cesare had withstood that farrago of gruesome lies about her lover in the country? He might be within a death-defying inch of reaching out and choking the life out of her for her apparent promiscuity and greed but, on the brink of murder or otherwise, he was ready to embark upon financial negotiation for her sexual favours.

Mina had never been more appalled or more shattered. It was not a compliment, but Cesare wanted her *that* much? He had been so cool, so controlled last night. This afternoon he was neither. She had never seen him out of control before. Involuntarily she was fascinated by the play of vibrant, strong emotions across his rawly handsome features. He was fighting a very close fight between a desire to kill her and a desire to—*oh*!

A flush of heat prickling across her skin, every muscle tightening, Mina dredged her attention from the explicit sexuality of the all-male gaze roaming hotly over her.

'I don't think I'm really your type,' she muttered weakly, beginning to wonder if she belonged in an asylum.

'Someday, somehow, perhaps when I have sated this obscene craving for your body, I will take this out on your hide,' Cesare swore, like someone making a blood oath over a grave. 'I will punish you for this filthy negotiation that reduces me to the level of an animal!'

Dry-mouthed on the feeling that she had foolishly unleashed a whole lot more than she could handle in that brooding Sicilian temperament, Mina backed to the window, still refusing to look at him, not trusting herself, not trusting him, feeling with every fibre of her body the passion flaming reckless fingers of fire into the atmosphere between them. 'Cesare...I didn't mean to——'

'To think I could have saved myself from this,' he grated. 'The first day when you walked into that interview I decided I could not possibly employ a woman whom I wanted to strip and fling onto the nearest bed!'

Helplessly her head flew up. She couldn't believe her ears.

'I gave you a nightmare interview...and you took it,' Cesare condemned with lingering disbelief at such unfeminine strength of will and staying power.

'You were trying to scare me off?' Mina questioned in a tone of revelation.

'I was a fool. I gave you the job.'

Mina's mouth curved downwards. He had been lusting after her from the start but he hadn't shown it. He had played a waiting game, doubtless entertaining himself with the prospect of her willing and grateful surrender at the end of his little game. Wham-bam, but not thank you, ma'am.

She had been as naïve as a lamb skipping into the slaughterhouse and she was exceedingly tempted to demand to know why he hadn't taken precautions. Considering that she had dissolved into mindless joy at his first kiss and he had been the experienced partner, she was still astounded by his reckless disregard for the consequences. Only then did it occur to her, for the very first time, that where Susie was concerned she had absolutely no regrets about that night. She could not imagine life without her daughter.

'But now, at least, I know the kind of woman I am dealing with!' Cesare asserted with driven savagery.

Dragged back to the present, she discovered that Cesare was now so close that she could feel the heat of him. Her spine was already in contact with the window behind her. 'You know nothing about me!' she protested shakily.

'You excite me—what else is important?' he said thickly, regarding her with sizzling intensity from the vantage point of his greatly superior height.

Her breasts were stirring, swelling. A heady languor was sweeping through her limbs, a betraying twist of high-voltage sexual awareness curling low in the pit of her stomach. But she fought every treacherous sensation with all her might, wild colour burnishing her openly dismayed face. 'You don't even like me . . . you called me a thief and a confidence trickster!' she gasped. 'How can you still——?'

'Desire you?' Cesare filled in, his hands settling down on her narrow shoulders with a pronounced air of finality. 'Sex is an appetite. If I'm tired, I sleep. If I'm hungry, I eat. If I'm——'

'Shut up and let go of me!' Mina was starting to tremble, a terrible fear stirring inside her as she was subjected to the magnetic pull of his smouldering gaze. Her head whirled and her body no longer felt as though it belonged to her. Don't you dare touch me——'

'You're scared of *this* . . .' With a blunt forefinger he traced the scooped neckline of her summer dress, his touch so light that it whispered across her skin, but it left a trail of fire in its wake, made her breath catch in her throat, made the blood in her veins pound in insane acceleration. 'Now isn't that an interesting discovery?' he murmured in a satisfied purr. 'You've got an Achilles' heel after all, *cara*. That steel trap of a brain can't control what I make you feel and naturally that scares you.'

'Don't——'

'Don't what?' In an indolently smooth movement, Cesare dropped his hands to the swell of her hips and swept her up into his arms, a primitive blaze of triumph firing his lancing gaze. 'Don't touch you because you're afraid I might realise how desperate you are for my caresses? Don't touch you because you might give yourself to me for nothing?' He flung back his dark head and laughed with hard satisfaction. 'And you will. With me, there will *be* no price!'

'Put me down!' she shrieked, a spasm of rage taking hold of her, breaking through the erotic spell he cast.

He kissed her. He kissed her until her heartbeat was a crashing thunderclap inside her ribcage. She fought the hunger he was inciting, wild with fear that he was right and she could not control her own treacherously susceptible body. But he kept on kissing her with a wild hot passion that bruised her soft lips against her teeth and suddenly, as he sent his tongue in a delving foray into the tender interior she had attempted to deny him, she was jolted by an uncontrollable surge of need that clawed cruelly at her, making her moan like a trapped animal in pain.

Her head was swimming with dizziness when he let her come up for air. She was as weak as an accident victim, quivering with shock. She was lying across his lap on her bed. Long brown fingers, dark against her pale skin, were engaged in flipping loose the pearlised buttons on the bodice of her dress. In horror at the sight, she clasped a small hand to his in an effort to stop him.

'No!' she gasped, stricken.

'You're mine,' Cesare muttered thickly, one strong arm closing fiercely round her to stress the assurance, and he simply shifted his hand smoothly from beneath hers and slid it beneath the parted edges of her bodice, slowly curving his fingers over the firm thrust of one unbound breast.

It had been so long since she had known such intimacy that her teeth clenched on the sweet pleasure-pain of her own helpless excitement, and in the interim her hand fell away. He tugged the dress open, exposing the smooth pale flesh he sought, discovering the delec-

table curves she had tried to conceal. With an unashamed groan of hunger he caressed a pouting pink
nipple with almost worshipping fingers, watching the bud
bloom into aching prominence.

Her eyes were closed. 'No...no,' she mumbled, lying
back against his arm, struggling madly to control the
electrifying response shooting through her in debili-
tating waves.

'Exquisite... Your body remembers me even if that
mercenary little heart doesn't want to,' Cesare murmured, his breath fanning her cheek and his fingers
playing with her unbearably sensitised breasts with erotic
mastery.

A throbbing pulsebeat of terrifying hunger was controlling her now. Her mind was a desert, a wasteland,
empty of every thought. Her entire being was centred
on a knife-edge of anticipation. As the moist heat of his
mouth engulfed a tender pink nipple, she gasped as
though he had thrown an overload switch, lost to everything but what he could make her feel. With every sure
caress, she was sucked deeper into a whirlpool of passion,
seduced by her own desperate hunger.

On some other level she was aware of the cooler air
that brushed her skin as her dress fell away entirely and
then he was laying her flat, crushing her mouth under
his with raw, unashamed hunger. Her hands swept over
his silk-clad back in sudden frustration, instinctively
seeking the satin-smooth skin she remembered. His
muscles rippled as he tautened and broke the connection
of their mouths.

Her glazed eyes opened on that shock of separation.
He was ripping off his shirt, and she remembered that
from before, but she heard no warning bells. Past and
present had merged indistinguishably. The pectoral
muscles of his lean, golden torso were hazed with a
sprinkling of ebony curls. Like someone in an hypnotic
trance, she focused on the blazing gold of his eyes and
sank ever deeper into his power.

'You are so beautiful,' he muttered, his accent roughening every syllable.

She wanted to return the compliment but she couldn't find her voice. She lifted a hand slowly and spread it against the warm wall of his chest, mesmerised by the power of her own craving and the thunder of his heartbeat below her palm. He bent his dark head, ran the tip of his tongue sensually along the full swell of her lower lip and came down beside her again.

'Cesare...' It was a whisper of surrender so complete that she melted to liquid honey making it.

He found her reddened mouth tremulously open in welcome and responded to the invitation with a savage drugging intensity which overwhelmed her. Her fingers smoothed through his silky hair, tracing his well-shaped head, joy singing through her veins. In one impatient movement his hand closed round the band of fabric at her narrow hips and wrenched it out of his path, tugging up her knees to facilitate the operation.

She shivered violently and twisted under the onslaught of his mouth as he parted her thighs and explored the hot, moist centre of her. Deep in her throat she emitted a low cry, gripped by an intolerable pleasure that made her burn and quiver and shamelessly crave more. With a raw groan of excitement that more than matched hers, Cesare knelt over her, ravishing her soft mouth one more time as if he was stamping her as his possession.

He pulled her to him with strong hands and instantaneously attempted to sink into her with one powerful thrust. There was a flash of momentary pain that made her bite down on her tongue and taste blood. Cesare muttered something in Italian, settled his hands on her hips and drove into her again, making her tender flesh yield more fully, and the sensation was so unbearably pleasurable that she moaned in shock and delight, for she had worked so hard at forgetting, had made herself forget, that most intimate moment.

But Cesare was inside her again in the place that was his alone, and she wrapped her arms tightly round him in acceptance and welcome, letting him teach her that primitive rhythm again as he moved with a raw power that dominated and drove, allowing her no surcease from the crazed spiral of excitement controlling her. She hit that promised peak of glory in an astounded sunburst of pleasure that tore her apart as she jerked mindlessly beneath the waves of climactic release, crying out his name with tears of ecstasy in her eyes.

Cesare came down on her, nearly crushing what life remained from her, and then swiftly slid on to his side in the confined space, with one arm clamping her back to his hot, damp body. Her cheek rested against a smooth brown shoulder and her nostrils flared on the warm, aromatic maleness of him. She was in a state not a hair's breadth from heavenly bliss and there still wasn't a single atom of activity in her brain.

His hand splayed across her lower stomach and then stilled, explored the fine seam of the scar he had come upon. 'What caused that?' he asked with sudden tension.

Mina's brain switched back on, all systems on red alert. Cesare was already flipping her over, evidently intent on examining the imperfection visually. But before she could attempt to snatch up something with which to cover a nudity that without warning now struck her as appalling he had achieved his objective.

Cesare had turned pale at one glimpse of her Caesarean scar. 'You've had surgery,' he breathed as she sat bolt upright, grabbed clumsily at her discarded dress and concealed herself behind it as best she could. '*Major* surgery——'

'No, only a little female thing,' Mina lied in desperation, evading his shocked gaze. 'It looks much worse than it is.'

'What was the matter with you?' he demanded tautly.

'I told you, something female and *private*—minor.'

'It doesn't look minor——'

'But it is and I'm sorry you find it so offensive,' she said wildly, ready to say or do anything to throw him off the subject.

'Of course I don't find it offensive but naturally I was disturbed,' Cesare asserted stiffly, 'and if that is the result of some minor female problem you must have had a third-rate surgeon!'

As he sprang off the bed, entirely unconcerned by his lack of clothing, Mina made no response. She was remembering the day of Susie's birth. The long labour that had eventually led to the necessity of a Caesarean section. What she remembered most clearly was the terrible sense of aloneness that day and the days which had followed before she was released from hospital. All the other women in the ward had had husbands or boyfriends, but she had only had Roger and Winona during all those endless open visiting hours and she had been so mortified by the sympathy of some of those women that she had chosen to kill Cesare off sooner than admit that her baby was the result of a one-night stand with a man who hadn't even wanted to lay eyes on her after it.

Yet even after that experience here she was *again* in a bed which Cesare had put her in. It was a devastating return to reality, plunging her down into a well of stark shame. Abruptly, seeking only to hide herself, she wrenched back the quilt and slid under it, turning on her stomach, burying her burning face in the pillow. She had betrayed herself. And she had no excuses to make in her own defence.

Four years ago she had loved Cesare and had mistakenly assumed that when he'd reached for her that night he'd wanted something more than sex. But she had found out the hard way that passion could give a dangerous illusion of intimacy. In her ignorance, she had read more into his behaviour than was there. This time, her savaged pride could fall back on no such misinterpretation.

A fiery desire drew them together, but in the aftermath they were separate again. Cesare despised her. Cesare had so low an opinion of her morals that he had swallowed whole all that nonsense she had spouted about having a weekend lover. It didn't really matter to him. All his ego had required was the humiliating surrender he could drag from her at will. He had told her that he would use her as once he believed she had dared to use him... and she had actually allowed him to do it!

How could she respond so wildly to a man she hated? What madness was in her that she could be guilty of such self-destructive behaviour? Four years ago, it had taken her months to rise above the conviction that she had been stupid and cheap and shameless. How long would it take this time? How could she live with the knowledge that in Cesare's radius she was every one of those three things? How could she live with the knowledge that when Cesare chose to reach out an arrogant hand to her she was his for the taking? Pain stabbed into her, sharp as a knife.

'I've changed my mind about you living with me,' Cesare imparted with flat emphasis into the thundering silence.

Hardly surprising, she reflected with a cringing shudder. He had already taken what he wanted and it had cost him the bare minimum of effort. Only an idiot would now go to the unnecessary inconvenience of moving her below the same roof! Seduction, soft lights and music or whatever had not been required. Just like the last time, Cesare had slaked his sexual hunger without any of the frills which other women probably took for granted. She took a masochistic satisfaction from lashing those unpleasant truths home to herself.

'Being waited on hand and foot by servants in luxurious surroundings would merely teach you all over again that you can get what you want out of life by using sex as a currency,' Cesare delivered, as if he were handing down a judgement from on high to the condemned scarlet woman about to be dragged out and whipped for the sin of being sexually available.

'I want you to leave,' a muffled voice said from the pillow. She wanted him to *go* before she started tearing her hair out and sobbing uncontrollably. It was her lowest hour.

'When you can establish to my satisfaction that every penny of that money is now gone, I will be prepared to assist you to move somewhere a little less like a hovel,' Cesare drawled coldly. 'But I am not going to keep you. You'll have to find work, some form of respectable employment where you will not be tempted by the opportunity to make money by deception.'

Stunned as all that sank in, Mina emerged from the pillow and encountered winter-dark eyes sharp as lasers. 'Doing what?' she probed in a wobbly voice of disbelief. 'Scrubbing floors?'

Cesare studied her with glittering cool. 'I don't care what you do as long as it's honest.'

'The reform package.' Hysteria clogged up her working throat. She struggled to keep it in but the mindless giggles tearing at her couldn't be restrained and spilt out, shattering the heavy silence.

With a vicious curse in his own language, Cesare came down on the edge of the bed and closed hard hands over her shoulders. 'Stop it!' he hissed.

'C-can't help it!' she gasped, but her overtaxed emotions somehow screamed to a frozen halt when she collided with the blaze of anger in his golden eyes.

'*Try*!' he raked down at her with lethal emphasis.

To her horror she felt the sting of tears and tore her gaze defensively from his. He had branded her a criminal, hounded her out of her job, deprived her of well-earned promotion, and she had rewarded that list of offences not with fury but with the gift of her body. Dear God, what was wrong with her? What was happening to her?

He sprang up again. 'Don't pretend that you didn't want me as much as I wanted you,' he murmured with cruel bite. 'And don't get me mixed up with any of your other bed partners. Crocodile tears leave me cold. I can see right through you——'

'You're blind!' Mina muttered strickenly, bowing her head over her raised knees.

'Stronger than you are. Harder than you are,' Cesare informed her crushingly. 'And a whole lot nastier when I'm crossed. Remember that and we'll get on fine.'

She heard the door open.

'Eight tonight. If you pull yourself together by then, I'll take you out to dinner.'

'You don't say,' Mina breathed in a deadened voice.

'You look as if you could do with feeding up——'

'The way you fatten a turkey up for the oven.' She felt physically sick, fully punished already for her own wanton lack of control in his arms. He would feed her and bed her. *Use* her until he got bored and, heaven knew, Cesare didn't stay with any woman for very long. He was determined to turn her into the equivalent of a sex toy he played with when he was in the mood, and she was willing to bet that he wasn't planning dinner anywhere where he might run into his friends or the Press.

'What the hell is the matter with you?' he suddenly shot at her.

She flinched. 'Nothing.'

'Stop looking so bloody pathetic, then!'

She curved her trembling hands round her knees. 'I'm tired, that's all,' she muttered, simply desperate for him to leave.

He bent down and tugged with disturbing gentleness at a strand of her tumbled golden hair. 'I didn't plan it this way,' he murmured, crouching down beside the bed. 'But I'd be a liar if I said I was sorry it happened. I don't want you to have any defences with me.'

'No,' she conceded unevenly, well aware that he had quite deliberately ripped all her defences away in one cathartic encounter, and that now he was on a high, callously unconcerned by what that same encounter might have done to her.

'Get some sleep... *Dio mio*...how could anyone sleep in this coffin?' he muttered with raw distaste.

He caught her hand and pressed a key into it with a grim sigh. 'You can stay in my town house but *only* for a couple of days. I'll send a car over to pick you up in an hour.' He straightened, strode back to the door again. 'I get in about six,' he murmured huskily.

And on this occasion she could read *his* mind. It made her cringe. She listened to the door close, a sob stuck like a giant boulder in her aching throat. Never, ever again would she allow him to do this to her. She would be out of here for good long before that hour was up, and so what if running like a rabbit was craven?

With the resistance she had to Cesare Falcone, only yet another complete fresh start would suffice. With him she was a tramp, wholly deserving of every insult he directed at her. It didn't matter that she had never been with any other man. Her pride and her intelligence had all the consistency of jelly around Cesare. But what mattered most of all was what he could do to her emotions.

She was lost in a terrifying sea of pain and drained of fight and anger. She could never recall experiencing such bitter turmoil. At the back of her mind she knew that, regardless of everything, running away wasn't going to take the pain of self-betrayal away. That pain was going to stay with her for a long time.

CHAPTER FOUR

'WHEN can you start?' Steve Clayton prompted cheerfully.

'Monday, if you like.' Mina chewed anxiously at her lower lip. 'Are you sure you really want me to work here?'

'Mina,' Steve groaned, 'maybe you're forgetting that I offered you the same job four years ago and you were too damned proud to take it!'

His mobile phone buzzed. Mina wandered over to the door, worriedly hoping that she had made the right decision in accepting the secretarial job she had once turned down...but secretly longed to accept. Times had changed, hadn't they?

Until their death in a car accident, her parents had rented a house on the Thwaite Manor estate. Steve was Baxter Keating's other grandson and Roger's cousin. The two boys and the Carroll twins had grown up together and dated as teenagers. The four of them had always been very close. There had never been any doubt that Roger and Winona would eventually marry and, although Mina was reluctant to recall the fact, Steve had expected that same commitment from her.

But it hadn't happened. Mina had outgrown her youthful crush on Steve and it had taken a great deal of courage finally to face him and tell him that truth. Roger and Winona had already been married and they had been as disappointed and hurt on Steve's behalf as Steve had been. Mina had felt horribly guilty that she had changed and Steve had not.

Her guilt had increased a hundredfold when Steve had asked her to marry him when she was pregnant with Susie. She had wished he hadn't asked, had felt even worse saying no, and had felt similarly unable to accept the job he'd then offered instead. The job would have been a lifeline but she had known that Steve still cherished notions of them getting back together again. In the circumstances it would have been wrong for her to accept his generosity. Steve was one of the main reasons why she had initially tried to make a go of living in London with Susie.

But times had mercifully changed, she reminded herself again. Steve had a steady girlfriend now. The passage of years had enabled them to return to their old friendship without undertones of what might have been complicating that relationship.

Mina jumped as Steve abruptly shouted, 'Susie! Get out of there!'

Spinning round, Mina saw a huge terracotta pot wobble alarmingly. A dark little head and a pair of far from intimidated golden-brown eyes appeared over the lip of the pot. Her daughter said a very rude word, a word few mothers would be hardy enough not to cringe at, hearing it issuing from the rosebud mouth of a three-year-old.

'Don't react.' Steve bit back a laugh as he saw the depth of Mina's horror. 'According to your sister, she'll forget it again if you don't make a fuss. But, as the culprit who said it within her hearing, Roger is never likely to use it again, even if he does drop a block on his big toe!'

Steve took her round the garden centre, pointed out the new extension with pride and completed the tour in his incredibly untidy office. 'Fancy some coffee?'

'I would have loved some but I'm baby-sitting this afternoon.'

'Rather you than me. Even on her own, Susie can be a handful. She has a will of iron and a temper like a tornado,' Steve remarked as he watched her daughter through the window. She was splattering back and forth through a pile of sand she had been scolded twice already for playing in.

'You were a bad girl,' Mina began, taking a short cut across the fields back to Thwaite Manor.

'I'm a good girl!' Susie told her with a flash of raw temper, and ran on ahead, thin, brown-as-nut legs twinkling under grubby white shorts, black pigtails bouncing.

Cesare's daughter and so agonisingly like him, Mina reflected painfully. The only thing Susie had inherited from her mother was her diminutive size. At three and a half, she was still tiny but, by virtue of her temper, highly unlikely to be bullied. She was bright, stubborn, manipulative...and often badly behaved, Mina conceded grudgingly.

Yet Roger and Winona had treated Susie exactly the same way as they treated their own brood of three. But John, Lizzy and Peter were quiet, easily handled children. Susie was different, a cuckoo in the nest with a far more volatile temperament. She had not received the firmer hand of discipline that she required. And whose fault was that? The buck stops here, Mina reflected guiltily.

'*Well*?' Winona demanded impatiently as Mina walked into the manor's large country kitchen.

'I'm starting on Monday.'

A vibrant smile lit her twin's face, so like yet so unlike her own. They were not identical, but as children the marked similarity between them had often fooled people into assuming that they were. In adulthood, the differences had become far more prominent. That had bothered Winona. She still lightened her hair to a shade as close as she could get to Mina's and wore it in the same style.

'Thank heaven you've finally seen sense! The four of us should go out for a meal and celebrate.'

'Five, surely—Steve's girlfriend would probably like to be included.' Mina tried not to sound dry.

Winona frowned. 'Jenny's away on a course right now. Anyway, what's it got to do with her? It's not as if they're engaged or anything... I'll book a table at the Coach——'

'No,' Mina inserted flatly.

'But why not?' Her sister already had the phone in her hand.

Mina sighed, wearily registering what her twin had contrived to hide until this moment. Incredible as it seemed to her, Winona still longed to see Steve and her twin reunited like Romeo and Juliet. 'I just don't think it would be a good idea.'

'What else happened with that creep Falcone?' Winona asked without warning.

Flames of colour washed over Mina's startled features. Caught unprepared, she had no time to assume the mask that concealed her inner turmoil. 'I——'

Her twin dropped the phone in shock. 'You *didn't* ... I mean, not again?'

Mina studied the surface of the breakfast-bar in the silence, her stomach cramping with sudden distress. She would not have told her sister but, directly faced with the question, she could not lie to her either.

'I'm going to do it this time,' Winona swore in a shaking voice. 'I'll take a gun out of Baxter's cupboard and I will go to London and shoot that bastard dead!'

'Winona——'

'Shut up,' her sister hissed furiously, this being the one subject capable of rousing her to temper. 'You protect him—you're *still* protecting him! Roger and I are perfectly willing to pay for you to take him to court and you won't let us——'

'I am not protecting him, I'm protecting Susie,' Mina whispered tightly. 'You know how much publicity such a case would attract and I wouldn't be able to hide her. Everyone around here knows I'm a single parent. I couldn't possibly take my daughter's father to court!'

'You slept with him—you actually slept with him again?' Winona suddenly demanded in complete disbelief.

Mina went white. 'I don't want to talk about it——'

'Are you still in love with him?' Winona muttered tautly.

Mina was rigid. 'Don't be ridiculous.'

'You're my sister and I don't understand you,' Winona complained in a tight, tremulous voice. 'Steve adored you. He didn't even object when you went off to college! He's handsome, caring and successful,' her twin enumerated, setting Mina's teeth on edge. 'If you have to make a fool of yourself with a man, why not do it with him? At least he would marry you!'

A shattering silence fell.

'I'd better hurry or I'll be late!' her twin muttered with guilty brevity, and rushed upstairs.

Two hours later, after clearing up the lunch dishes, Mina sank down on a seat beside Baxter, who was snoozing on an old wooden lounger on the lawn, his straw hat tipped over his face.

'Been getting the riot act read again?' he enquired, making her jump because she had believed he was asleep.

'Where did you get that idea?'

'I could hear Winona screeching from the hall.' The old man sighed. 'You'll be glad to move into Dempsey's cottage in the autumn. You and Susie need your own corner.'

'Yes.' Her cheeks burning, she was wondering how much Baxter had overheard.

The children were at the far end of the garden, playing in the tree-house Roger had built. It was a beautiful day, but for once the sunlight failed to lift Mina's spirits. It had been two weeks since she had left London. She couldn't eat and she wasn't sleeping much better. The quiet of the countryside had failed to work its usual magic.

'I'm very fond of your sister, but she's had life easy,' Baxter sighed. 'She married her childhood sweetheart at nineteen and never had to earn her daily crust. Everything she ever wanted was handed to her on a plate: her husband, her home, her children. Remind her of that reality the next time she starts on you.'

'Winona's been very good to me——'

'Not when she continues to ram that gormless grandson of mine down your throat! I could have told the lot of you when you were sixteen that you would never marry Steve. You didn't fancy him!'

A stifled sound escaped Mina. Sometimes, Baxter disturbed her. He saw so clearly, pierced right to the heart of the matter.

'That was as plain as the nose on my old face. But because Steve looks like Roger Winona can't understand your astonishing lack of good taste!'

'I hurt him,' Mina whispered unhappily.

'You'd have hurt him a great deal more if you'd let yourself be pressured into marrying him . . . Is that a car I hear?'

Mina turned abstracted eyes on the sweeping driveway at the same moment as a car appeared through the dense shrubbery which screened the manor's gates. It was a Ferrari, a silver one. Mina lurched upright on legs which suddenly felt like rubber, a sick sense of shock paralysing her to the spot.

'Who is it?' Baxter grumbled, tipping off his hat and squinting.

Cesare sprang out of the car. He didn't even bother to close the door again. His entire attention was pinned to the little tableau of sunbathers on the front lawn. He strode across the grass, every long biting stride expressing ferocious purpose. He flipped off his sunglasses, digging them into the pocket of his jacket. Sheathed in a cream summer-weight suit of exquisite cut, black hair gleaming in the sunshine, he looked outrageously exotic.

'The Mafia have arrived,' Baxter muttered in a tone of somnolent amusement.

Mina clashed with shimmering gold eyes across a distance of ten feet. It was like being grabbed by the throat.

She was so horrified by Cesare's descent that she couldn't unglue her tongue from the roof of her mouth.

'I'm taking you back to London with me,' Cesare enunciated with a flash of even white teeth. 'Don't bother packing, just get in the car! I'll deal with you later...'

Baxter dealt him a highly entertained look of intense interest and actually roused himself sufficiently to sit up as Cesare strolled closer with the slow, silent intent of a predator tracking his prey.

Mina read the dark fury suddenly locking Cesare's facial muscles taut, and belatedly recalled the lies she had told in London. She surged into sudden motion as Cesare angled his smouldering attention on Baxter. 'And as for *you*,' Cesare intoned with vicious bite on a quite visible wave of clench-fisted frustration as he viewed the older man, and Mina imposed herself between him and his quarry, 'if you weren't halfway into the grave already, I'd bury you!'

'*Cesare!*' Mina exclaimed.

He thrust her out of his path. 'Mina is young enough to be your granddaughter!'

Baxter surveyed Cesare with amused blue eyes. 'Is he always like this?' he enquired of Mina, who was unmistakably cringing, colour running up her throat into her cheeks like a banner. 'Or has somebody been telling the poor chap whoppers?'

'Cesare...I lied——'

'About what?' he raked at her.

The engine of the Ferrari suddenly fired into motion. His ebony head spun.

'Oh, my God!' Mina gasped as she saw the perky red bow just visible through the window on the passenger side. Susie was in the driver's seat. As Cesare raced across the lawn, she flew in his wake.

Cesare reached the Ferrari first, ducking down and emerging with a kicking, screeching Susie, who hadn't seen him coming and who had been thoroughly enjoying herself. Even as Mina looked on in a state of mute horror, she saw her daughter bend her head and sink her teeth into the hand attempting to restrain her.

'*Dio*! You little animal!' Cesare grated as he released his tiny squirming burden and incredulously studied the teeth-marks on his hand.

Susie said her rude word. She knew it was offensive and she flaunted it. She squinted up at Cesare in a temper and slung it like a sailor squaring up for a fight. Cesare stared down at his daughter with appalled distaste and strode out of reach. He met Mina's stricken eyes across the roof of the Ferrari. 'What a revolting child,' he breathed, brushing at the smear of dirt on his previously immaculate jacket. 'Filthy as well!'

'What's revolting?' Susie's voice warbled.

Mina was terrified to speak because Susie wasn't yet aware of her presence on the other side of the car. Her niece and nephews were lurking in a tight group several feet away, drawn by Susie's shrieks. John, a sturdy six-year-old, inched forward and told Susie that she should apologise.

'Susie never says sorry,' Lizzy complained.

'Sorry,' Peter said. A quiet little boy, almost exactly the same age as Susie, he had already formed the somewhat irritating habit of apologising for his cousin.

'Not sorry.' Susie gazed up at Cesare, having tailed him round the bonnet.

Ignoring her with supreme cool, Cesare sent Mina a fulminating glance. 'Why are you standing there like a statue? And what did you lie about?'

Susie tugged at his trouser leg. 'Not sorry,' she said again, wanting a reaction.

'Go away,' Cesare grated in exasperated aside, and pulled free.

Susie's bottom lip wobbled alarmingly. 'You're not nice.'

'Nice would be wasted on you.'

From somewhere, Mina regained sufficient self-possession to say, 'John, take Susie back to the tree-house.'

As her much bigger cousin began to trail her away, Susie burst into floods of tears and screamed for her mother. Mina's fingernails dug painful crescents into her palms as she ignored that call that tugged painfully at her heart-strings.

'What did you lie about?'

'How did you find me?'

'Ways and means. I asked you what you lied about,' Cesare bit out with lancing impatience.

As Susie's sobs receded into the distance, Mina breathed again. All that was on her mind was getting rid of him again as fast as she possibly could. Did he know that this was her sister's home? She didn't even think he knew she had a sister, and it was wiser to keep him in the dark.

'Baxter's not my lover—actually, he's only a guest here,' Mina improvised on the spot. 'I'm staying with friends.'

'And which one of the *friends* is the lover?'

Mina coloured hotly and ignored the question. 'I want you to leave, Cesare.'

'I'm not leaving without you,' he told her harshly.

Her head jerked in the direction of the gate as she heard another car approaching. It was Steve's Range Rover. To say that Mina's nerves had already withstood about all they could stand would be an understatement. She experienced a cowardly urge simply to cut and run as she watched Steve slow down and suddenly brake to a halt as he recognised the man standing beside her.

'Please leave,' Mina whispered in desperation as a car door slammed.

'What the hell are you doing here, Falcone?' Steve demanded, his tanned face flushed with angry disbelief as he strode forward.

'Cesare is just leaving,' Mina said loudly.

'Introduce me,' Cesare murmured flatly, scanning the burly blonde man with dark-as-night narrowed eyes.

'Clayton—Steve Clayton,' Steve supplied with aggression, moving forward to plant himself by Mina's side. 'And if you don't get off this property you're going to get those fancy togs messed up!'

'You think so?' A chilling smile curved Cesare's sensual mouth.

The tension that had immediately sprung up between the two men shattered Mina. She glanced in horror from one to the other.

'I think so,' Steve said. 'You look like a male model.'

'Steve, please...' Mina hissed, watching Cesare's gaze blaze with what could only be described as sheer pleasure. It dawned on her that he had come here to knock seven bells out of the other man she had so stupidly and recklessly assured him existed in her life. Faced with Baxter's frailty, he had been balked of his prey. Faced with Steve, he could be as physical as he liked.

'I've been waiting for this for a bloody long time!' Steve shot at her hotly.

'Mina's returning to London with me. Go and sit in the car and cover your eyes, *cara*. I won't be long.'

Since she had absolutely no hope of persuading Cesare to back down, Mina turned back to Steve. 'This has nothing to do with you.'

'Nothing to do with me? He took you away from me four years ago!' Steve thundered at her, and even though that wasn't true, even though she had broken up with him eighteen months before she'd even gone to work for Cesare, she realised for the first time that that was exactly how Steve had chosen to deal with that part of the past.

'And I'm about to do it again,' Cesare drawled.

'Stop it...*both* of you!' Mina was appalled by the scene that was developing. 'The children could see you... Have you gone crazy?'

Cesare tensed but, a split-second later, Steve lunged at him. Mina didn't quite know how it happened but

Cesare side-stepped the attack at speed and punched him in the stomach. As Steve grunted and doubled up, Cesare strode past him and clamped a hard hand on Mina's arm. She was shaking all over.

'Get in the car,' he told her between clenched teeth. 'Because if that guy gets up again I'm going to rip him apart with my bare hands!'

'I can't...I'm looking after the kids!'

'Go for a drive, Mina. Let tempers cool,' Daxter suggested in wry intervention from the sidelines.

Mina rebelled. Men! she thought furiously. 'I haven't the slightest intention of getting into a car with him, and if there's any more fighting I'll use the garden hose to cool tempers!' she asserted witheringly.

Cesare simply picked her up and dumped her like a parcel into the passenger seat of the Ferrari. He had swung in beside her before she had recovered from the shock.

'Let me out of this car *right now*!'

'You created this situation—you deserve everything you get,' he delivered harshly.

Mina fumbled frantically at the door, but it was locked. Cesare braked as the car reached the shelter of the shrubbery at the gates and turned to her, blazing golden eyes biting into her. 'How long have you known Clayton?' he demanded.

'None of your business——'

Cesare reached out a lean brown hand and speared his long fingers into her tumble of golden hair, preventing her retreat. The ferocious anger he had been controlling leapt out at her, shortening the breath in her throat. 'Don't tell me that,' he warned her not quite steadily. 'I am trying very hard not to lose my head.'

The atmosphere was explosive. Her amethyst eyes were entrapped by gold threat. She lost colour and trembled and yet a twist of wholly primitive excitement ignited her senses on another level. It was two weeks since she had felt like that. It was like life after near death, sudden, piercingly sweet and joyous and, no matter how hard she fought that extraordinary feeling, it sent the blood racing madly through her veins.

'You had no right to come here,' she said breathlessly, struggling to think straight.

'No?' With his thumb he traced the trembling curve of her full lower lip and she shivered violently in reaction.

'I'm calling your bluff. I want to see the evidence you have against me,' Mina told him jerkily.

'No. That's confidential and safely stowed away,' he spelt out.

'Then take it to the authorities,' Mina advised in bitter frustration. 'I won't be blackmailed. Do your worst——'

'What about my best?' As he leant forward, he let his thumb softly intrude between her lips, seeking out that damp, warm interior. 'Don't you know what I do best?'

Her heartbeat was thundering in her eardrums, an almost terrifying languor stealing over her, weighting her limbs. She snatched in a breath, feeling the stirring heaviness of her breasts, the sudden frantic plunge down into intense sexual awareness. Involuntarily snared by mesmeric golden eyes, she was held fast by something far stronger than she was. She wanted him to touch her so badly that it hurt, it literally hurt to be denied.

'It doesn't even have to be my best,' Cesare murmured thickly, dense black lashes screening his gaze to a sliver of hard gold as he scanned her feverishly flushed face and unwittingly pleading eyes. 'The one thing you ever gave me that was honest...why? You can't control it. But I can——'

'Can you?' Mina was in another world, one where she felt far more than she thought. Her hand lifted of its own volition, shyly smoothed along his strong, clean-shaven jawline, fingertips softly brushing a high cheekbone. Her nostrils flared on the warm maleness of him. That close, it would have been sensory deprivation not to touch.

He dipped his dark head and trapped her fingers with his mouth before she could reluctantly drop them again. Her eyes squeezed shut on a wave of unbearable excitement as he sucked first one finger and then another and her breath rasped in her dry throat, liquid fire running through her quivering body, melting every bone to boiling honey. She was poised on the edge of an erotic anticipation so intense, it consumed her.

'Cesare...' She curved into him, aching for closer contact.

His hand tightened painfully in her hair. Her lashes flew up, crashing her into molten gold demand. '*Dio*! I want to be inside you,' he muttered with a shuddering savagery that shook her to her very depths. 'But afterwards I'd wonder whether you turn on like this for Clayton as well. And I expect you do. After all, he looks the type likely to offer you a wedding-ring. I'm not surprised you didn't want me to find you.'

'It's not like that...' It was an effort to think, an enormous effort. Her whole body was aching with a need strong enough to drain her of all self-will.

'Sex with me or security with him,' Cesare drawled with derision.

'Steve is not my lover——'

'Only another string to your bow.' Cesare vented a rough laugh, his strong features laced with innate cynicism and contempt. 'How many more strings do you have? You lead a double life, Mina. Haland and your humble little job, which would undoubtedly have become extremely lucrative but for my intervention, and down here... Is that his house up there?'

Mina was savaged by the reminder of his image of her. How could she have forgotten for one moment how he saw her? Yet she had forgotten—she had forgotten so completely that, but for his greater control, she would have let him make love to her right here in the car. Her skin crawled with shame at her inability to withstand the desperate hunger that Cesare could evoke within her at will. 'No.'

'Maybe he isn't rich enough yet for you to retire— maybe he's simply an insurance policy on a back-burner. Who owns that house?'

'I'm not telling you.' She wrapped her arms round her still trembling body, suddenly feeling cold, dimly acknowledging that she was suffering from shock.

'I can find out. You know that.'

'Please leave me alone,' Mina suddenly breathed. 'Just go away and forget you ever knew me!'

'I'll do that *after* I've had you in my bed for a while,' Cesare spelt out with hard emphasis.

'I won't let that happen again!'

'You're so hot for me, you won't be able to help yourself.'

Every scrap of colour drained from her cheeks. The savage pain of humiliation engulfed her. In Cesare's eyes she would always be a confidence trickster and a tramp. Dishonest and promiscuous and greedy for money. He despised her but he got an electric charge out of using sex to reduce her to emotional and physical rubble. 'I'm not what you think I am,' she whispered tightly. 'And I don't know why you hate me so much.'

'Someday, if I'm feeling very cruel, I might tell you.' His lean face was as hard as iron as he said it.

He expelled his breath in a sudden hiss and rammed the car into reverse.

'What are you doing?' Mina gasped in consternation.

'You're so desperate to get me away from here, I want to know why!'

'*No!*' Mina protested, her voice breaking up with stress.

Cesare flicked her a grim glance. 'You brought this on yourself, *cara*. Your two worlds are about to collide!'

'It's Baxter's house!' Mina told him in rush. 'Baxter Keating. Steve is his grandson——'

'You told me Baxter was a guest. Are you a compulsive liar?' Cesare sent her a glittering look of anger.

'I'm not lying this time. I just don't want another scene.'

'Or maybe you're scared in case Clayton finds out a little too much about you,' Cesare suggested unpleasantly.

'Don't go back to the house!'

Cesare sent her an insolent smile. 'What's it worth to you?'

Her skin burned. 'No...'

He skated a long forefinger very slowly down her slender thigh and looked at her with sizzling challenge. Mina went rigid, every physical sense leaping back on to red alert with a raw immediacy that horrified her. He had stopped smiling, his strong face taut, his eyes flaring. He curved his hand over her knee and reached for her again, without warning bringing his mouth smashing down on hers hard enough to hurt.

Only it didn't hurt, it thrilled. Electrifying excitement engulfed her in a tidal wave. His tongue drove between her lips, searching her out, tasting her, emulating a far more intimate possession with an explicit sexuality that overwhelmed her. It felt as if the top of her head was flying off. Her fingers dug forcefully into his shoulders, dragging him closer because she wanted more, so much more, and the hunger he had unleashed on her was a wildly potent provocation.

Cesare tensed, momentarily holding himself back, and then her tongue flicked against his in an enticement that was entirely instinctive and, with a raw groan of need, he ravaged her reddened mouth with potent hunger. Suddenly she was no longer upright but lying back. His hand slid up one trembling thigh, wrenching the dress out of his path.

She was out of control, her breath sobbing in her throat, her heart racing. She clung to any part of him she could reach, her fingers clutching at his hair, the back of his neck, splaying against the silk-clad heat of his taut abdomen, scratching down his long spine, clothes, always clothes getting in her way, driving her mad with frustration.

Cesare suddenly stilled and dragged his mouth from hers. Then she heard the noise. Someone was banging on the window and shouting. Her heavy eyelids lifted very slowly. A fire-alarm couldn't have dredged a faster response from her. Her body was on another plane, her mind absent without leave.

Cesare swore in guttural Italian, a dark flush accentuating the fevered glitter of his eyes as he registered their surroundings. '*Cristo* . . . you make me do crazy things!' he condemned as he abruptly swung back into his seat.

As he did so, Mina clumsily began to sit up. *She* made *him* do crazy things? The eternal Eve syndrome, she reflected bitterly. Only then did she see and recognise the red car parked and evidently abandoned in a hurry to one side of the gates . . .

It was her sister's car. Sheer horror turned Mina white.

While Cesare, awesomely in control at having been surprised in such a situation, inexplicably lowered the window on the driver's side when he could simply have driven out on to the road, Mina attempted to shrink backwards and conceal herself behind him, panic taking hold of her as Winona's shaking and outraged voice filled the car.

'Do you think this is a lovers' lane?' Winona was shrieking in fury. 'How dare you park in the entrance of my home and behave like that? It's disgusting!'

CHAPTER FIVE

SICK with horror, her sole ambition escape without de-tection, Mina hissed at Cesare in a frantic whisper, 'Drive off, for goodness' sake!'

Dear heaven, how could she have sunk this low? In broad daylight in a car parked on a driveway where anyone could have come upon them! But she had no doubt that the police moving them on would have been infinitely preferable to Winona. Her pride in tatters, her sense of humiliation overpowering, Mina sat there like a graven image just waiting for the axe to fall. She couldn't understand why Cesare hadn't driven off or why he was so silent.

'Oh, my God,' Winona suddenly gasped, and peered into the car, fixing stricken and incredulous eyes on Mina and then switching them to Cesare in belated recognition. 'Get out of his car!' she screeched full blast.

'At first glance, the resemblance is really quite startling, but you're not identical. Sisters?' Cesare queried in a staggeringly controlled tone, only his thickened accent betraying that he was not quite as in control as he wanted to appear to be.

'Did you hear me, Mina?' Winona positively shrieked. 'Get out of his car!'

'Twins.'

'At least I didn't bag the hysterical one,' Cesare murmured flatly.

'Who the hell are you calling hysterical?' Winona screamed at him, banging a fist on the windscreen.

With admirable cool, Cesare shot the car into reverse again and began backing up the driveway. 'So your sister lives here too. Interesting.'

'She's married to Baxter's other grandson.'

'Why did she go crazy when she saw me?' Cesare probed.

'It really would be better if you let me out here and left,' Mina managed tremulously as Winona's car roared up the drive and raked to a halt beside them. It was a relief to note that Steve's Range Rover had gone. He must have left by the back lane.

'But I wouldn't miss this for the world. It's like one of those mystery weekends in a country hotel.' Cesare watched in apparent fascination as Winona hurled herself out of her car and raced past the Ferrari like a maniac. 'She's pretty, not beautiful like you. Does she envy you?'

'Not at all.'

As Winona vanished into the house, Mina clambered out on cotton-wool legs. 'Please go,' she pleaded without a lot of hope.

Cesare slid out and slammed the door again with an air of pronounced finality. He straightened his tie, smoothed back the hair her fingers had tousled. Then he stilled, his dark features tautening. 'You're not married to Clayton, are you?' he suddenly demanded.

'Of course not!'

'Of course?' Cesare loosed a sardonic laugh. 'Where you're concerned, *cara*, nothing would surprise me!'

Thinking about Susie, she hoped he kept that in mind. If she had been a cat she would have used up eight of her nine lives over the past hour. Now she was hanging on to her last life by the skin of her teeth.

'May we enter the house?' Cesare enquired gently.

'I would much rather you left.'

'And miss this wonderful opportunity to meet your family?' Cesare drawled satirically.

The front door was wide open. From the breakfast-room Winona could be heard shrieking at somebody. Cesare winced. 'Somebody needs to throw a bucket of cold water over her.'

'She hates you. What do you expect? My family know what you've accused me of! They know *why* I'm out of work again as well!' Mina threw at him.

'The injured innocent act,' Cesare murmured, unimpressed, flicking her a grim glance. 'I assume you play the martyr for their benefit. Don't get carried away with your role.'

'Why don't you just get out of here?' she suddenly demanded a whole octave higher.

'Not you as well,' another voice groaned.

Mina spun round. Roger had appeared in a doorway, his working clothes making it clear that he had come in from the haymaking out on the estate. 'What the blazes is going on? Steve damned near hit the tractor on the back lane and I come back here and find Winona trying to get a gun out of Baxter's cupboard... She's hysterical!'

'I suggest you don't mention that fatal word,' Cesare drawled.

Roger stared at him, frowned, and drove a hand through his sweat-streaked blonde hair. He looked at Cesare, then back at Mina, and sighed. 'All of a sudden I see the light. I'm Roger Keating, Mina's brother-in-law, Mr Falcone.'

'Don't you dare be polite to him, Roger!' Winona snapped, stalking out into the hall. 'Tell him to get out!'

'Winona,' Roger muttered, tight-mouthed with embarrassment. 'Let's at least try to be civilised about this——'

'Civilised? This is the bastard who ruined my sister's life!' Winona railed in a shaking voice. 'He's caused this family nothing but misery——'

'Don't say any more... please,' Mina broke in tautly.

'If it weren't for you, Steve and Mina would be married by now!' Winona condemned as she glared at Cesare with loathing. 'Steve was even willing to take on your child but Mina was too bloody proud to let him do it, and now, just when everything is finally beginning to go right for them, you show up again!'

Without looking at anyone, Mina swung round and walked back out of the house, rigid-backed and sick inside. The dreadful silence followed her. And then she heard Cesare rake back with, '*My* child?' His tone was raw with disbelief.

Winona burst into tears, belatedly realising what she had done.

Mina sank down on the bench on the south wall of the house. The heat of late afternoon did nothing to lift the deep inner chill sinking into her very bones. She folded her hands together tightly. She could have told him herself but wild horses wouldn't have dragged it from her. After what Cesare had put her through four years ago she would have cut out her tongue sooner than let him know that she had given birth to his child nine months later.

That birth had been the last in a long series of humiliations inflicted by him and when she had realised that she did not have the strength to surrender her daughter to adoption and the more secure background that would then have been hers her sole consolation had been the belief that Cesare would never, ever know that Susie existed.

A long dark shadow blocked out the sunlight.

'Tell me it's not true,' Cesare urged her fiercely.

Mina fixed her attention on the gravel, her eyes burning. 'I told you to stay away from me——'

'Knowing I would keep on coming! I don't believe you had my child...'

'No problem. Get back in your car and drive away,' Mina advised in a wooden undertone that masked her increasing turmoil. 'That's what I wanted right from the first moment I laid eyes on you again.'

'It's impossible!' he asserted roughly.

'I wish it had been.' But that wasn't quite true. She did wish it and she didn't wish it. She adored Susie and had made considerable sacrifices to keep her but she had also discovered the hard way that single parenting included a lot of guilt and inadequacy. In addition, she had had to rely on her family to enable her to give Susie a decent home and for someone as independent and proud as Mina that had been a constant source of self-reproach.

'There were four children,' Cesare began without any expression at all.

Three blonde, one black-haired... and 'revolting'. Hysteria clogged up Mina's throat. She was waiting for the awful truth to dawn on him. In the space of five ghastly minutes, Susie had contrived to expose her every flaw. Her temper, her tenacity, her aggression.

'The one who bit and swore?' Cesare prompted not quite levelly.

The silence stretched and smouldered with the strength of his incredulity.

'Are you telling me that that dirty little creature is *my* child?' he suddenly slammed at her with raw ferocity. A hard hand closed over her shoulder without warning and literally hauled her upright. 'I asked you a question!' he roared down at her, giving her a little shake that made her hair fly round her distressed face.

'But you don't really want the answer, do you?' she burst out.

Abruptly he thrust her back from him and strode away a couple of paces before restively swinging back to her. He was very pale, his hard bone-structure harshly prominent beneath his dark skin. 'She didn't look old enough.'

'She'll be four in December. She's small, that's all.'

Cesare's narrowed dark gaze held hers with sudden chilling menace. 'She looked neglected...'

Mina was violently off-balanced by the charge. 'N-neglected?'

'*Madre di Dio*... if you are telling me the truth and that child is mine...' Cesare's expressive mouth compressed into a savage bloodless line '... who the hell has been looking after her while you've been in London?'

'My sister——'

'That shrieking harpy?' Cesare blistered back at her.

Mina turned white at this unfamiliar description of her sister. 'Winona loves Susie!'

'But she *hates* me!' Cesare shot at her with black fury. He raised a brown hand and slashed it through the air. 'If that little girl is mine——'

'Will you stop saying that?' Mina interrupted painfully. '*If* she's yours! Nobody brought you here to pin Susie on you! You brought yourself here and refused to leave. If Winona hadn't lost her head, you still wouldn't be any the wiser——'

'And why is that? Why, if you were pregnant, didn't you contact me?' Cesare demanded in a driving undertone. 'Why do I only find out by accident?'

Mina lifted her chin, fighting to control the wobble in her voice. 'I should think that's obvious. I didn't want you to know. I didn't want your financial help. In fact I didn't want anything more to do with you. I didn't ever want to see you again. I owed you nothing after the way you treated me!'

'But what about what you owed the child?' Cesare intoned with scorching emphasis. He watched her strained face tighten and uttered a harsh laugh. 'No, you didn't think about her. I don't think you think about her very often——'

'How dare you say that?'

'She's dirty, foul-mouthed, improperly supervised and desperate for attention. That doesn't say much for you as a mother, does it?'

'You only saw her for a few minutes. You don't know her,' Mina whispered, stricken, appalled by his censure. 'She's a tomboy but she has a bath every night. She only says that one bad word...'

'Forgive me if I'm not too impressed.' Cesare looked at her with bitter condemnation. 'So Susie is the trouble I would be digging up which I wouldn't want to handle? Why did you have her? Was she your insurance policy against prosecution? You were ready to use her to protect yourself, weren't you? After all, she hasn't clipped your wings much. You dumped her down here and simply got on with your life!'

White-faced, Mina's distraught gaze clung to his fiercely clenched features in growing horror. 'It wasn't like that. I left her here because I couldn't afford anywhere decent to live and I knew she was well looked after and safe here with my family——'

'Where is she?' Cesare glanced around expressively, an ebony brow rising. 'You don't even know, do you? She could be out on that road under a car!'

'She's too scared to walk over the cattle grid!' Mina lifted a trembling hand to her throbbing brow, wondering what she had done to deserve this nightmare. Whatever response she had expected from Cesare it had not been an immediate catalogue of scathing attacks on her parenting skills.

'She runs wild... my child, my daughter whom you tell me I had no right to know about! Who the hell do you think you are, to make a decision like that?' Cesare shot at her with unhidden savagery.

Pale as paper and trembling, Mina whispered, 'You treated me like——'

'You deserved!' Cesare cut in before she could complete the sentence. 'But I did attempt to see you again after that night because I was concerned that my irresponsibility might have had repercussions.'

Shaken by the reminder, Mina looked away from him.

'When I couldn't find you, I called myself a fool for imagining that you would have taken such a risk. I assumed you had guarded yourself against pregnancy before you got into my bed,' he revealed, his delivery suddenly icy cold, the anger tamped down and rigorously controlled. 'It never crossed my mind that you might choose not to inform me of your condition. But then, why should you have done? You didn't need my money to support her. Your wonderfully understanding family took responsibility and left you free——'

'That isn't how it was!' Mina protested with a sob in her voice.

'*Per amor di Dio . . .*' he ground out thickly. 'You have given me such a shock, I feel as if the ground is rocking under my feet!'

Mina was in tears. She felt like a target and he was the one throwing the knives, his aim deadly in its cruel accuracy. Too much had happened in too short a time space; too many agonising emotions had been unleashed and right now she was in the eye of the storm, powerless to control them. But when she looked at him, registered by the lines of savage strain etched into his clenched features that he was suffering an equally powerful emotional conflict, that somehow hurt even more than what she was feeling.

And finally she saw into herself, would have done anything to shield herself from that private viewing but what she saw could not be buried again. An anguished understanding of her own pain had flooded her. She *still* loved him. That was the only reason why Cesare could still hurt her to this extent. It was the worst time imaginable to make that discovery. The acknowledgement that she still loved him devastated her.

She collapsed down on the bench again, weak as water, and lowered her aching head. He hated her and she wanted to put her arms around him! She wanted to tell him she was sorry even if she didn't know quite what she should be sorry for as yet. How the heck could she defend herself feeling like that?

'I need time to think this over,' Cesare admitted flatly and then he threw her entirely by simply walking away.

She stared after him with despairing eyes and slowly closed them as the throaty purr of the Ferrari faded away into the distance. He was devastated too and she had never seen him in that state before. But then finding out you were a father four years after a one-night stand wasn't something that was covered by any book on social niceties. Worst of all, it was not a situation which Cesare was able to control, and if there was one field in which Cesare excelled it was controlling everything and everybody within his radius.

He despised Susie's mother and he hadn't been much more impressed by his first meeting with his daughter. But Cesare was very family-orientated. He wasn't the kind of man who was capable of forgetting that he had a child because it didn't suit him to have that child. He took his responsibilities seriously. Hadn't she seen him in action with his obnoxious brother, Sandro?

He looked after Sandro, had given him a fancy title in Falcone Industries to keep him happy and stuck him in a very large office where, even with the very limited powers at his disposal, Sandro still managed to get himself into one mess after another...messes which Cesare cleared up and covered up. Why? Sandro was family. Sandro had had endless excuses made for him.

Why was she thinking about Sandro? But she knew why. Her last memory of Cesare's brother was scorched into her bones. The morning after that night she had spent in Cesare's arms she had wakened alone and wandered out of the bedroom half dressed, and had discovered to her mortification that the voice she could hear speaking on the phone belonged not to Cesare, but to his brother...

Sandro had asked her out the very first day she started work at Falcone Industries. She had turned him down, had had no plans to date anyone she worked with. In any case, Sandro was creepy and she hadn't been in her job a week before she'd realised that the majority of the secretarial staff felt the same way as she did about the boss's kid brother.

In Falcone Industries, Mina had entered an exclusively male executive clique and she had been shaken by their hostility. Even the other PAs would have cut off their hands sooner than help her out when she was trying to find her feet. She had walked into a plum job which some of them had applied for and the word had been that Cesare had employed her simply because she was easy on the eye. The next rumour had been that she was sleeping with the boss.

Cesare had not stepped in to help her. He had sat back and let her get on with it, sink or swim. But he had stopped the filthy jokes and the foul language in the boardroom, probably because she suspected that there had never been such offensive talk until her arrival. They had tried to treat her like an errand girl and for a while she had been foolishly obliging, hoping to make friends and show that she was not too big for her boots.

'You only make coffee for me,' Cesare had told her one day. 'You only run messages for me. Learn to say no to everyone but me.'

How long had it taken for her to fall in love with him? His sophistication and his looks had initially intimidated her and he hadn't been easy to work for. The first time he had shouted at her she had locked herself in the loo and fought back childish tears. The next time she had shouted back... and after a stunned pause he had stunned her by laughing. He had fascinated her right from the beginning. He was brilliant in business, intensely competitive but not a workaholic. If he worked hard, he also played hard and she had been staggered by the speed with which women came and went in his highly visible social life.

By the end of the first month, Mina had known she had three problems. One was that Sandro Falcone was refusing to take no for an answer and becoming increasingly unpleasant. The second was that she was passionately attracted to Cesare. The third was career-orientated. Cesare flew round Europe on a regular basis but he didn't once take her with him; he took her subordinate instead, leaving Mina in London.

'Did I say I would take you abroad with me?' he had responded when she had finally picked up the courage to query that omission.

'Well, no, but——'

'Maybe this job isn't working out for you?' He had dismayed her by looking as if that idea appealed to him.

The second month he had become more short-tempered. In fact the more overtime she'd worked, the harsher he'd become. They had been spending a great deal of time alone together. By then, Mina had known that she was head over heels in love. The third month, the evidence of all the other women in his life had vanished. She would look up and find brooding golden eyes fixed on her and the air would hum but she had blamed herself for that awareness and feared that he suspected her feelings for him.

And then, that final night, they had been in the penthouse apartment at the top of the Falcone building. Everyone else had left but she had been finishing off transcribing her notes. He had offered her a glass of champagne and then, quite out of the blue, those golden eyes had suddenly shimmered down at her. 'I surrender,' he had muttered rawly, and he had grabbed her and kissed her breathless.

The glass had dropped out of her hand. He had kept on kissing her. She didn't even remember how they had got to the bedroom. Cesare had given a very good impression of being as out of control as she was yet she did recall that he had taken immense care not to hurt her the first time they made love.

'I never mix business and pleasure,' he had said afterwards. 'But this is different.'

And as far as meaningful conversation had gone that had been that. By the time she had got her mouth open, he had been making love to her again. As for pillow-talk concerning a deal he had recently closed, she had fallen asleep in the middle of it, waking up late into the morning when she should have been at her desk, appalled that Cesare had not roused her before he'd left. She had also been the victim of her own doubts and insecurities, painfully conscious that she could not recall Cesare saying a single word which might have allayed her fears that she had made an ass of herself.

Sandro had spun round and surveyed her with startled disbelief when she'd come running out of the bedroom, not even sure what time it was and hoping to catch Cesare before he departed for Hong Kong.

'So Cesare hit paydirt,' Sandro had finally sneered after a long silence. 'You're a joke, Mina. And let me tell you something else: you backed the wrong horse. My brother doesn't believe in office nooky. He thinks it's bad for the old team spirit. The day before you started work here everybody was warned off you!'

'I don't believe you,' she had mumbled.

'And now he has had what nobody else was allowed to have he'll dump you so fast and hard your head will spin! Cesare always goes by the book.'

Birdsong pierced her concentration. Blinking, in a daze, Mina was dragged back out of the past and she focused on the fading sunlight and the garden but she didn't see them. She was still reliving the unutterable humiliation of that encounter—Sandro's smirking face, his suggestive voice pawing over something which had until that moment been precious and oh, so private. He had made her feel grubby but she hadn't believed that Cesare would behave like that, had initially refused even to entertain the idea that he could have swept her off to bed on nothing more than a lustful impulse.

'Mummy?'

She glanced up. Susie was sidling along the wall towards her, her small face stiff with uncertainty. Mina's throat closed over and she opened her arms. Susie flew into them, locking her arms round her mother's throat in a stranglehold, with all the fierce affection that was the other side of that temper of hers.

'Sorry,' she sniffed.

Mina smoothed the dark head buried against her shoulder, wanted to squeeze her to death with the force of her own disturbed emotions.

'Not be bad any more,' Susie promised.

'Darling, you're only bad sometimes.'

'I get cross.'

'I know,' Mina soothed. 'But you mustn't bite people.'

'When you going on the train?'

Mina swallowed back the thickness in her throat. She had told Susie repeatedly over the past fortnight that she wasn't going to be leaving on the train again but Susie couldn't quite accept that yet. She had been accustomed to Mina's departures for so long. Was Cesare right? Had she done everything wrong with Susie? Should she have buried her wretched pride and asked for his help? But she had envisaged so many even more humiliating scenarios when she had considered telling Cesare that she was pregnant.

After all, her knowledge of Cesare then had been formed on the basis of that one fatal night and his subsequent conduct. She had pictured him denying that he was the father of the child she was expecting or, perhaps even worse, furiously and resentfully accepting responsibility and making it very clear that she was now an even more unwanted embarrassment.

But now she knew that Cesare had sacked her not because she had shared his bed but because he believed that she had acted dishonestly and betrayed him. In a veil of pain, she recalled his accusation that she had betrayed him 'as an employee *and* as a lover'. Yet, even crediting that, Cesare had still sought reassurance that she was not pregnant, had tried to contact her, find her...

Dear God, what a mess, Mina reflected wretchedly. If only she had the power to turn the clock back and know what would have happened and how he would have behaved had he found her! Maybe the whole mess could have been sorted out then, but would it really have made any great difference in the long run?

True, he might have given her financial help but it was not as though he had loved her or even been interested enough to toy with the idea of a continuing relationship with her. For Cesare that night had been a mistake and on that basis Susie had to be an even bigger mistake in his book.

'Hi...' Mina smiled but there was an air of uneasiness about her as she hovered in the aisle of the giant greenhouse.

Steve straightened from the pricelist he was checking and dealt her a sullen look which made her heart sink. 'Why didn't you join the rest of us for dinner at the Coach last night?'

'Sorry; I didn't feel much like going out.'

The past two days had been very tense for Mina. She had been waiting for the phone to ring, the doorbell to shrill. But there hadn't been a single word from Cesare, only a silence which could be read in half a dozen ways and which had merely increased the burden of her anxiety. How *did* Cesare intend to deal with the discovery that he was the father of a three-year-old daughter? Or indeed did he intend to deal with it at all?

'I didn't feel much like socialising either but I went.' Steve moved closer without warning and reached for her hands, holding them in a tight grip, preventing her retreat. 'How the hell could you go off with Falcone like that?' he demanded furiously. 'You made me look a right fool!'

Mina had tensed. 'I——'

Unhidden bitterness had darkened his blue eyes. 'Seeing him brought it all back. If it hadn't been for him——'

'Cesare had nothing to do with our break-up!' Mina protested, finding that her worst apprehensions had been justified. Cesare's descent had reanimated Steve's resentment and she had little doubt that his unreasonable attitude had been encouraged by her sister over the dinner the night before.

'I really loved you——'

'But you've got Jenny now,' Mina whispered tautly, looking up at him with pain-filled eyes, inwardly begging him not to lay that guilt-trip on her as well.

'You are so very beautiful.' Steve lifted a hand and touched a glossy strand of her golden hair. 'So perfect——'

'Mina...?'

Both their heads spun round. Mina froze at the sight of Cesare where he stood in the doorway. More casually dressed than she had ever seen him, he sported cream chino trousers and a black open-necked shirt under a light jacket, but, for all that, the entire outfit was exquisitely tailored, stamped with Italian designer chic. He looked gorgeous. Her heart skipped a beat. Her mouth ran dry.

Surprise had made Steve loosen his grip and she freed her other hand from his belatedly, her skin burning. She could have screamed at the fate which had decreed that Cesare should witness this particular encounter. She knew exactly how he would translate what he had seen. Now he would probably think she had been lying when she had said that Steve was not her lover.

'Baxter told me I had just missed you. Susie showed me the short cut.'

Susie peeped round Cesare and emerged, untouched by the raw tension holding all three adults taut. She had a teddy bear clutched in both arms. In the simmering silence she poked at the bear and it started to sing, its mouth and eyes moving. A nervous giggle convulsed Mina's throat. But then she encountered Cesare's hooded dark gaze and all desire to laugh was instantly banished. That look was like an ice-cold hand on her spine.

'I'll see you,' she said to Steve.

'I'm not going to bite again!' Susie carolled, offering up her bear for admiring inspection. 'And I said thank you! Do you know I have a granny who loves little girls?'

'A granny...do you?' Mina's response was faint as she followed her daughter back out into the fresh air. For some reason she hadn't been prepared for Cesare arriving with a present for Susie, signifying a clear desire to further their acquaintance, but she was even less prepared for hearing Susie cheerfully talking about Cesare's mother as her grandmother.

'Perhaps you will tell Susie who *I* am as soon as possible,' Cesare suggested drily.

'Don't you think that would be a bit premature?' Mina murmured, struggling to conceal her consternation.

'Not at all, considering that the news will be coming to her three and a half years too late.'

Mina shot him a startled glance as she traversed the stile that led from the garden centre car park into the field. Cesare held her gaze with icy cold challenge and she lost colour, apprehension suddenly filling her. He had changed. And she felt that change as strongly as though he had slammed a door in her face. He was detached from her in a way that was frighteningly new to her. Finding out about Susie had done this. She had sensed that chill from the moment he first looked at her. It intimidated her.

'Are you saying that you want to play a part in her life?' she prompted in a strained voice, striving to imagine what her life would be like with Cesare dropping in and out of it as he pleased.

'A permanent part.'

'Really?' Mina tautened, and a long silence fell.

She had expected Cesare to make some crack about the scene he had interrupted but he didn't and she was relieved. Steve's behaviour on its own was a sufficient worry. If he was still attracted to her, how could she work for him? Maybe he had only been reacting to the past, which had so suddenly been raked up; maybe within a few days his current response to her would melt away again... but what if it didn't? Mina did not want to be guilty of coming between Steve and Jenny.

'We'll talk inside,' Cesare decreed as he strolled into the house. He bent down as Susie tugged at his trouser leg. 'I'll see you later,' he murmured with more warmth than Mina would have believed possible, considering the mood he was in.

She pushed open the door of the rarely used drawing-room. 'I'll make some coffee,' she said breathlessly.

'Forget the coffee,' Cesare advised with grim emphasis.

As he closed the door, Mina folded her arms and wandered over to one of the sash windows. She felt cornered. He was going to offer her money towards Susie's support. What else could he want to discuss? She found the concept unutterably humiliating but possibly she would have felt able to be less emotional and more practical had she not been in love with him, she acknowledged unhappily.

'I won't waste your time or mine with trivialities,' Cesare asserted. 'The bottom line is that I want my child.'

Mina spun back to him, her fine brows drawing together.

'And I would prefer to get her without a fight,' Cesare delivered in the same cool, controlled tone.

'I don't understand...' Mina whispered shakily, skimming suddenly damp palms down over her thighs.

'I can give her a great deal more than you can.'

Mina could feel the blood draining from beneath her skin, shock turning her flesh clammy.

Cold dark eyes rested on her without compassion. 'I'm willing to legally adopt her.'

Mina licked her dry lips in a flickering motion. 'You can't be serious.'

'She's my child and I want her——'

'The implication being that I *don't*?' Mina gasped. 'You're not talking about the take-over of some company, Cesare, you're talking about my daughter!'

'And mine,' he reminded her, with a flash of deep anger briefly illuminating his winter-dark gaze to pure gold. 'But you were quite content to ignore my rights for over three years—why do you then expect me to be so much more generous when it comes to yours?'

'I'm not talking about rights, I'm talking about feelings,' Mina muttered unevenly, still too shaken by a development she had not foreseen even in her worst nightmares. He wanted to take Susie away from her. She couldn't believe it, didn't want to believe it.

'Are you trying to say that you considered mine?'

Mina flushed and sank down on the edge of a nearby chair, her knees too wobbly to hold her upright. 'I didn't know you would have any feelings... I mean, if you didn't know...' she stumbled.

'But I do know now and I have not the slightest intention of leaving you in sole possession of my daughter,' Cesare informed her flatly.

'You're trying to punish me.' Mina hadn't meant to say it out loud but she was in such conflict, she let the thought escape.

An almost imperceptible darkening of colour accentuated the hard slant of his cheekbones. 'I want what is best for my child and I am not leaving her in this house to live on your family's charity!'

'Baxter's offered me a cottage which will be vacant this autumn. Susie and I will be living alone and you can visit as much as you want... or I could even bring her up to London!' Mina suggested in a frantic rush, willing to do just about anything to placate him until she could get her thoughts back under control.

'I want more than that small share offered at the point of a gun,' Cesare derided.

'You want blood... well, I am not giving Susie up!' Mina sprang upright, sudden fury powering her, her amethyst eyes brilliant as jewels. 'And what sort of man are you to demand that? I love her very much and whether you appreciate it or not she loves me too, and not all the money in the world is likely to compensate her for losing her mother!' she shouted back at him with clenched fists.

Cesare lifted a broad shoulder and shrugged with Latin cool, his intent scrutiny a glittering sliver of unreadable gold below luxuriant lashes. 'You have a point.'

Disconcerted by the swiftness of his agreement, her emotions all churning about wildly inside her, Mina drew in a deep, shaky breath of relief.

'If you're not prepared to give her up and you feel that she would be emotionally damaged by such a separation,' Cesare drawled smoothly, 'then I have little choice but to offer you a home as well.'

Mina blinked rapidly. She was sure she hadn't heard him right. 'P-pardon?'

'Trailing you through court for custody would be a deeply unpleasant experience for all of us and very upsetting for Susie,' Cesare murmured very softly. 'And even though I'd throw everything I've got at you, I might not win. A foreigner in a British court, a father suing a mother...my lawyers were reluctant to go beyond a fifty-fifty estimate of my chances of success.'

Mina viewed him with stricken eyes and ended up sinking back down on the chair. 'Your l-lawyers?'

'Naturally a man in my position would take legal advice.'

Nasty little cramps were pulling at her stomach. Her head was pounding. She was sick with horror at the facts he was reeling off with complete cool.

'You see, I feel very strongly about this,' Cesare told her quite unnecessarily.

'Yes,' she conceded numbly.

'But accepting you along with Susie would be the wiser alternative from the child's point of view.'

It took Mina at least thirty seconds to untangle and absorb that statement. 'I don't quite understand what you mean by that.'

'If I married you, I would have all the time in the
world to get to know my daughter,' Cesare drawled
without any expression at all. 'And Susie would have
the benefit of two parents.'

CHAPTER SIX

'IF YOU married me?' Mina parroted in a voice that even to her own ears sounded strangled.

'In addition, Susie would have my name. That is important to me. She would share my home. That is also important to me. And she would have her mother,' Cesare enumerated coolly.

She noticed that he didn't include Susie's having her mother as being important to him. Clearly that could only be seen as an advantage to Susie. Shell-shocked by the suggestion that they marry, Mina swallowed hard. 'But——'

Cesare let her get no further. 'You can't live with me without a wedding-ring, not with Susie around. She would be branded as my illegitimate child and I don't want her to bear that label.'

'No?' Mina was flat out of anything else to say. But she had an extraordinarily powerful desire to slap him hard and see if the ice cracked. Cesare at his most unlovable, she reflected, trying to inject a little humour into her growing sense of mortification. How to propose marriage like a business deal with Susie as the most desirable asset!

She knew Cesare. He would have cut his throat sooner than offer her marriage on any other terms! He didn't want to marry her but if marrying her was the only sure way to acquire Susie, who had had a meteoric rise from revolting status, he would bite the bullet.

'Susie deserves the very best that I can give her. My parents did that for me. I will do it for her,' Cesare imparted with grim emphasis. 'If I did anything less, it would be on my conscience forever. So call me when you've decided what to do.'

In disbelief, Mina watched him stride out of the door. She flew upright and chased after him, bubbling with frustration and anger. 'Cesare?'

He swung gracefully round on the steps, his strong face hard and impassive.

With difficulty, she held back her anger. 'Don't you think this is something we need to discuss in more depth?'

'*Perché*...why?'

'I think that has to be the stupidest question you have ever asked me,' Mina protested helplessly.

'What more is there to say?' he breathed tautly. 'The court or the church. The choice is yours.'

For a split-second she glimpsed the rage he was struggling to conceal behind the cold front of detachment. His ferocious tension sprang out at her. Abruptly, he turned from her again and strode towards his car.

She was outraged that she had to run after him again. But he spun back before she could even speak. 'How could you keep my child from me? How could you *do* that?' he demanded rawly.

Mina fell back a step, shattered by the force of his embittered stare. 'I didn't think you'd want to know...' she whispered painfully, savaged by that ringing condemnation.

'What do you know about me?' Cesare spread both hands wide in a sudden violent movement that fully expressed all the emotion he had been suppressing. 'What have you ever known about me?'

'Probably only what you choose to show,' Mina conceded grudgingly. 'And between you and me and the gatepost, Cesare, that is not a lot!'

'*Dio mio*...what is that supposed to mean?' he slashed back at her.

Mina bit into the soft underside of her lower lip, wishing she had kept her mouth shut, but remembered pain stirred when she thought about the night on which Susie had been conceived. Cesare was not verbal about his feelings. So presumably he hadn't had any particular feelings that night. That had only been sex. She ought to be grateful he hadn't told her any lies but one of her own most painful memories was telling him that she loved him. And not just once either...she had been so overcome by what had happened between them, she had been floating on cloud nine.

She compressed her lips. 'It's not important, but when you talk about marriage,' she muttered, 'that *is* important.'

'From Susie's point of view,' Cesare stressed. 'I'm putting her needs before my own. For me, it is not a question of personal choice. It is a very basic instinct that I should take full responsibility for my own child...and what real decision is there for you to make? Am I not offering you the lifestyle you have always wanted?'

Deadly pale, Mina lifted her head high. 'You don't know what I want!'

With a rough laugh of disagreement, Cesare swung into his car.

'If I'm so greedy for money, Cesare, ask yourself why I didn't tell you about Susie years ago,' Mina suggested furiously. 'Legally you would have had to support her and I could have lived very nicely off the proceeds. So tell me, why didn't I do that?'

A smouldering silence stretched. She could see the frustration currenting through him. He could not explain such an inconsistency and that merely served to infuriate him more. He muttered something vicious in his own language.

'You can't answer that one, can you? Or what about why I would be plotting and planning to enrich myself by deception in a boring nine-to-five job when I could have forced you to keep us both?'

'Give me time and I'll work it out!' Cesare swore with vehemence, shooting her a look of derisive brilliance, refusing to back down. But she knew she had made her point and if anything illustrated the intensity of Cesare's emotional conflict in recent days it was his failure to see that point for himself. She had had no need to struggle for survival or plan to defraud a charity, not while she stood in possession of the child of a very wealthy man. Susie could have been the gravy train she rode for her own selfish benefit.

'What did he want?' Winona demanded from behind her.

She was grimly amused by the low profile her twin had kept during Cesare's visit. Her sister was still recovering from the sensation that she had made a fool of herself forty-eight hours earlier. 'He...' Mina hesitated '...he suggested that we consider getting married,' she finally completed.

'He did *what*?' Winona looked stricken, the way you looked when the enemy did something entirely unpredictable.

'For Susie's sake.'

'Considering that he can't keep his hands off you in a public place, it has to be for his own sake too!' Winona told her witheringly but with something less than her usual venom.

But Mina genuinely did not think that. Cesare did not want to marry her. He would not even have mentioned marriage had it not been for Susie's existence. He might lust after Mina but on every other level he despised and distrusted her. And what sort of a marriage could you have on that basis?

'I didn't think he would want to marry you,' Winona confided abstractedly, and Mina knew that Cesare's stock had suddenly gone up a hundredfold in her sister's eyes. To give her twin her due, Winona had never once voiced the embarrassment she experienced over her sister's unmarried motherhood, but the prospect of a wedding-ring tidying up that unfortunate fact of life quite clearly had immense appeal.

Mina didn't bother to mention Cesare's references to lawyers, courts and custody battles. In her opinion that had merely been Cesare putting on the pressure and testing the water. As soon as he had established that there was no question of her being prepared to give Susie up voluntarily, he had proffered the marriage solution. Everything else had been an intimidating lead-in to a proposition he fully expected her to accept. Working for Cesare had been an education. In a tight corner he never put his cards on the table.

His methods outraged her. She did not appreciate being approached like a hostile take-over bid. Yet Cesare had reacted to the discovery that he was a father in a far more responsible and positive way than she had expected and she could not think that there was an alternative to marrying him, not when she took her own feelings into consideration and added them to the undoubted benefits for Susie. Her daughter needed a father, a home of her own and security. Mina felt guilty that she hadn't been able to supply those things.

And she was equally well aware that, no matter how angry Cesare made her, she would rather be with him than without him, but a marriage made only on the basis of a child's needs was a tall order. In recent days she hadn't had time to dwell on her own emotions but just as she knew the sun would rise in the morning she knew she loved Cesare, and it was that fact which more than anything else would prompt her to accept his proposition.

Surely within the closer relationship of marriage Cesare would begin to realise that he had misjudged her? She would ask for the evidence which he insisted he had. No, she would not ask, she would *demand* that evidence. Somehow she had to clear her name. She refused to contemplate the idea that that ambition might not be satisfied.

'Mina?' The strained quality to Winona's call made Mina glance up from the toys she was tidying in the sitting-room. 'Cesare's here.'

'*Again?*' she gasped in astonishment.

He appeared in the doorway. Instant wish-fulfilment, she reflected dazedly, running her amethyst eyes from the crown of his dark head, down over the rest of his long, lean body, the most inescapable sense of possessiveness powering through her. He took her breath away, even though he looked uncharacteristically frazzled round the edges. His black hair was slightly tousled, his jawline blue-shadowed and he wasn't wearing his jacket.

'I was wondering,' Cesare breathed tautly, faint lines of strain indented between his nose and his set mouth, 'if you would like to dine out this evening?'

It was already after six. Thrown by his unexpected arrival for the second time in the same day, Mina didn't say anything; she simply stared and nodded. She got up off her knees, suddenly understanding his presence. He wanted to know her decision, evidently had not been able to wait even a reasonable interval to give her time to make up her mind. As the children clattered in a clump through the hall behind him, his head jerked round in obvious search for Susie. He heard the teddy bear first. Their daughter skipped in and grinned up at him.

Cesare couldn't take his eyes off her. Something mean and envious twisted briefly inside Mina and she was instantly ashamed but at that moment she would have given anything to have the power to extract the same answering smile from Cesare on her own behalf. In addition there was a bonding beginning to take place which had nothing to do with her.

Susie was not accustomed to much in the way of male attention. Visitors and relatives made more of her cousins. Susie was well aware that she was a bit of an outsider in this household. She had spent the entire day brandishing that bear, painfully proud that for once she had got a present exclusively for her.

'You're a very pretty girl.' Cesare hunkered down on a level with his daughter.

Susie beamed. 'Not bite again,' she said in reward.

'I'll get changed,' Mina murmured, deciding to leave them alone instead of hovering like a gatecrasher, uncertain of her welcome.

At the door, she paused without looking back. 'I've decided.'

'What?' Growling tension accented the question.

'The marriage solution would be the best for you-know-who.'

There was a long silence. Why did she get the idea that it was smouldering? But she wouldn't have turned her head and shown her face for a thousand pounds. 'Cesare?'

'I'll make the arrangements,' he murmured without any expression at all.

Winona cornered her on the upper landing. 'There's a limo with a chauffeur out there!' she stage-whispered, impressed to death. 'Do you want to borrow something to wear?'

'No, thanks.'

By the time she came downstairs again, dressed in a casual floral skirt and blouse, Cesare had already told her family that they were getting married. Roger had opened a bottle of wine to celebrate, patently determined to make up for the deficiencies of Cesare's welcome on his previous visit, and Winona had for some reason changed Susie into a white broderie anglaise dress which had once belonged to Lizzy. Her sister's motivation soon became clear.

'I thought that Susie should dine out with us,' Cesare drawled, skimming Mina with flat, unreadable dark eyes.

And if there had been any prospect of Mina thinking that Cesare felt that they had anything personal to celebrate, it simply died there. She had wanted and expected to be alone with him and even admitting that to herself in the face of his cool indifference cut her to the bone.

*   *   *

Mina flicked a glance at her shiny new wedding-ring, her soft mouth tightening before she went back to surveying the Sicilian countryside through the window of the limousine. They appeared to be travelling right into the very heart of the island..

Cesare had said they would be staying at his home. Since he had offered no further details, Mina had chosen not to ask for them. But the landscape of rolling agricultural land had changed. The climbing road was now passing through thick forests of pine and eucalyptus trees, dappled sunlight and then shade playing through the silent car.

The silence was like a razor rasping against tender flesh. No doubt it was her nervous tension which translated the atmosphere as one of menace. Her imagination was playing tricks on her, she told herself. The worst Cesare could do was continue to ignore her. In fact she marvelled that, feeling as he so evidently did about her, he had decided to make such a trip.

They had married in the local church early that morning. The deed had been done very quietly. Cesare had not invited a single relative or friend to attend and although Mina had not been sorry to miss out on Sandro, whose reaction to their marriage would surely not have been a joy to behold, she had felt that that omission said a lot about how Cesare viewed their marriage.

Not that she should have required that further education after the past three weeks, she thought painfully. Cesare had driven down to Thwaite Manor several times but all his attention had been reserved for his daughter. Mina had been consistently sidelined and held at a distance. When she had agreed to marry Cesare, she had not expected to be treated like some sort of hanger-on, only to be tolerated in Susie's presence!

'He really is desperately fond of her already, isn't he?' Winona had said with rather forced cheer, doing everything but heave an open sigh of relief on Mina's behalf when Cesare had actually accepted her twin's offer to hang on to their daughter for the duration of their trip to Sicily.

Evidently Cesare could not forgive her for keeping Susie's existence a secret. And, though he had decided that marriage was the only acceptable solution to Susie's needs, the necessity of doing so had outraged him. Only six weeks ago, Cesare had exploded back into Mina's life, determined to punish her for what he saw as her betrayal four years ago. But Susie had come between Cesare and the revenge he desired.

He had been forced to put his daughter first. The concept of revenge had been thrust willy-nilly into the bounds of impossibility. And, even more infuriatingly, he had then found himself marrying a woman he saw as greedy and dishonest. As Mina sat there it slowly sank in that unwittingly or otherwise she had turned the tables on Cesare with a vengeance. The biter had been bit, not only denied retaliation but forced to make sacrifices and concessions of his own.

'We're here.'

Something in Cesare's voice made Mina look at him first. It was a note of raw energy that she hadn't picked up in his vicinity for three long weeks. She was even more staggered when the formerly grim line of his mouth suddenly curved into a wolfish smile. He had been so cool, so controlled for so long, it was like watching a very bland actor step down off the stage and instantaneously switch back to his own vibrant personality.

Thrown by the strange imagery assailing her, Mina might have kept on staring had not something of what lay before them stolen her attention. The limo was crawling up a steep, wooded hill to what looked like a vast stone fortress.

'Your home is a ... castle?' Mina queried in a faint voice.

'For three centuries Castello del Falcone has guarded this valley from all intruders. I usually fly in and out by helicopter but I believed you would find the long car journey on these sadly poor roads...shall I say...educational?'

Bemused by his sudden loquacity, Mina opened dry lips, keen to respond to the smallest olive-branch. 'The scenery was beautiful.'

'But this is a most isolated valley. In winter the road out is frequently impassable. You will have noticed that it is some hours since you saw a town. The nearest village is several miles away. Our staff live in.'

Amazed by the amount of information being freely showered upon her, Mina suddenly believed that she understood what had achieved his radical change in mood. Cesare was coming home, and if coming home could warm him up to this extent she was delighted! Obviously he was very proud of the *castello* and his family's long association with its history. So she did not remark that those gaunt grey walls rising from their craggy heights were distinctly intimidating.

The limo passed beneath a giant gateway and into a cobbled courtyard charmingly embellished with urns of flowers. 'How lovely,' Mina sighed with appreciation, climbing out of the car into the lengthening shadows of evening.

'A shame it is so far from the nightlife and the shop-till-you-drop streets of Paris and London.'

'Yes, but as somewhere you can come to relax and unwind...' Mina scanned her surroundings with fascination '...it's wonderful!'

'I hope that feeling has staying power.'

Mina was so relieved that he was talking to her again, she glowed. Pride told her that she ought to be cool but she loved him too much to hold spite and was painfully aware that there was some excuse for his animosity. Cesare had every right to feel bitterly angry that he had been denied knowledge of his daughter but she prayed that he was now coming to terms with what after all was an unalterable fact. Mina was more than willing to meet him halfway in the hope that a few days alone together might result in the building of a firm foundation for their future.

'I love country life,' she told him cheerfully.

Cesare smiled sardonically. 'Even in winter?'

But she wouldn't be here in winter, she almost said, and then a plump little woman in black came out to greet them and be introduced as his housekeeper, Maria. She didn't have a word of English but her beaming smiles were sufficient welcome.

'I'll have to learn Italian,' Mina laughed, feeling ridiculously bubbly but her relief at Cesare's improved spirits was so immense, she couldn't help it.

'You'll be able to learn at your leisure.'

Why did she keep on getting the impression that Cesare was talking tongue-in-cheek? She thrust the suspicion away again, telling herself not to be silly. Cesare was her husband now and for once he was being remarkably civilised in not giving way to the more volatile strains of his temperament. After all, Susie would not be happy if she sensed the dissension between her parents and presumably he had finally reached that conclusion.

'Let Maria take you upstairs. We'll dine at nine,' Cesare drawled.

From the great hall wound a magnificent marble and wrought-iron staircase. Everywhere Mina looked she saw the evidence that the *castello* had been gently and sympathetically modernised by succeeding generations of Cesare's family. She followed Maria up the grand stairs but then they traversed a stone passageway which was frankly medieval in its simplicity. A door was cast wide on a large oak-panelled bedroom rejoicing in the baroque splendour of a massive and extravagantly carved bed and it was like leaping forward again into the eighteenth century.

A door in one corner led into a charming bathroom cunningly contrived out of a turret room. Alone, Mina explored her surroundings, a faint frown-line etched between her brows as she registered that Cesare evidently did not intend to share this room with her. Her cheeks colouring, she reminded herself that an hour ago it would not even have occurred to her to think that he had the smallest intention of making love to her ever again. He hadn't even kissed her since the day he found out about Susie.

On more than one occasion she had told herself that his indifference mattered to her not at all. But the truth was...the truth was that never in their entire relationship had she felt more painfully rejected or less able to defend herself. Mina had had time to search out her own failings in recent weeks and she was unhappily conscious that four years ago she had put her own pride ahead of what might have been best for her daughter. It was blatantly obvious to her now that no matter what Cesare might think of her he would always have put Susie's needs first.

A long bath relaxed her. She emerged from the bathroom and was disconcerted to find a youthful maid laying out clothes for her on the bed.

'But these aren't mine.' Mina touched a filmy piece of silk and lace lingerie with uncertain fingers and frowned at the shimmering luxury of the exquisitely fashioned black evening gown. 'Where are my clothes?'

The younger woman looked anxious. 'You no like, *signora*?' She hurried over to one of the vast wardrobes and cast the door wide, revealing a sea of multi-coloured garments.

Startled, Mina opened another door and met a similar sight. Drawers were packed with lingerie, shelves with sweaters and on the floor were neat rows of shoes, every item clearly brand-new. Comprehension assailed her. Cesare had bought her a new wardrobe. She was astonished. Here and there she saw a glimpse of her own clothing, plain and inexpensive items which must have been carefully unpacked and hung while she had been in the bath. There was no comparison between those garments and the designer apparel which Cesare had purchased.

The black dress which would leave her shoulders bare was seductively gorgeous. After gently dismissing the maid, Mina dressed herself and swept her hair up in her favourite soft Edwardian knot. She pirouetted in front of a full-length bevelled mirror and ran an admiring hand over the rich fabric which rustled softly with her every movement. Her slim shoulders looked very white rising from the fitted bodice.

She felt like a million dollars wearing silk against her skin. She loved beautiful things but she had never had the wherewithal to indulge herself. She was really touched that Cesare had made such a gesture and without fanfare, without even mentioning it ... taking her quite by surprise. She reminded herself that she had entered a different world, one where people dressed for dinner every night, not just when they had guests, and thought that it had been very thoughtful of Cesare to foresee that reality and quietly take care of it for her.

As soon as she was ready, she hurried breathlessly downstairs, her high heels ringing across the tiled floor of the entrance hall. All of a sudden she couldn't wait to see Cesare. A manservant followed her and as she hesitated, not knowing where to go, he pushed open a door.

The sun was setting in a magnificent blaze beyond the tall, narrow casemented windows at the far end of the room. Cesare was standing there, the light glinting off his ebony hair, a white dinner-jacket accentuating his stunning dark good looks. He took her breath away when what she had childishly wanted to do was steal his but she couldn't read his gaze in that light.

'You look every bit as pleased with yourself as I thought you would,' he murmured softly.

Her skin flushed, her eyes brilliant, she took the comment at face value. 'The clothes were a wonderful surprise,' she told him in a rush. 'Thank you.'

'Don't mention it. If my wife were poorly dressed, it would reflect on me,' Cesare told her drily. 'And undoubtedly there will be times when I entertain here. It would be embarrassing if someone mistook you for one of the servants.'

Mina recoiled as if he had slapped her in the face. She heard him speak to the manservant whom he addressed as Paolo. A brimming glass of champagne was offered to her on a silver salver. She grasped it with an unsteady hand.

'What shall we drink to? The institution of marriage?' Cesare said with a sardonic smile. 'Or your withdrawal from the world you love so much?'

'I beg your pardon?' Mina couldn't help the tremor that interfered with her voice. In the space of a few sentences, Cesare had ripped away her illusion that he was softening towards her.

He strolled gracefully out of the strong light into greater clarity. His lean golden features were taut with grim satisfaction as he absorbed her bewilderment. 'You may not be dressed like one but you are about to embark on a life as constricted as that of a nun in a closed order,' he imparted softly.

'Have you been drinking?' Mina whispered, that being the only explanation she could find for such an extraordinary forecast.

Cesare threw back his dark head and laughed with unashamed amusement. 'You never did ask where you were going to live,' he reminded her. 'So now I'll tell you. You will live here.'

'*Here* ...?' Mina echoed uncertainly.

'I'm not taking you back to London.'

'But I assumed that we would be living in Lon——'

'You assumed wrong. I can run my companies from anywhere. Technology makes that possible. I'll have to make occasional trips but you'll remain here keeping the home fires burning and devoting your energies to being a mother to our daughter,' Cesare spelt out. 'A role which will no doubt challenge you to the utmost.'

Mina gulped down champagne purely to wet her dry mouth. She gazed at him as if he had confessed to sudden madness, her amethyst eyes wide with incredulity. 'If this place is as isolated as you said it was, it's not suitable for Susie!' she objected shakily, that being the first thought that came to mind.

'It's extremely suitable. I subsidise a very modern and well-equipped nursery and combined primary school in the village four miles from here. The younger generation were being forced to move away because of the lack of proper educational facilities for their children. The estate requires workers and the old people need their families near them. We are a mutually dependent community.'

'Susie doesn't even speak the language, for goodness' sake!' Mina gasped, taken aback by the speed and assurance with which he had answered her protest and the uncomfortable awareness that the subject was obviously something Cesare had already considered in depth.

'And should she not learn? This is my home and therefore her home as well,' Cesare responded. 'Children of her age pick up another language very quickly. She will grow up bilingual.'

Belatedly, Mina understood his cracks earlier about the *castello's* distance from the nightlife and fashionable boutiques. Evidently he believed that such things were highly important to her and he was determined to deprive her of any such frivolous pursuits. Actually, Mina had not been talking for effect when she'd said that she loved country life but she sensed that Cesare was threatening her with an isolation more akin to imprisonment than anything else.

She was appalled. Did the idea of marooning her here, far from her family and everything familiar, appeal to him that strongly? Was he trying to punish her for putting him in a position where he felt he had to marry her to gain proper access to his daughter? Was he so bitter that he was determined to do everything possible to make their marriage an unhappy one?

'Dinner,' Cesare murmured, pressing a lean hand to her taut spine and pushing her gently towards the door. 'You're in shock, aren't you?'

'I can't think of one good reason why you should be behaving like this!' she exclaimed helplessly. But she could think of a whole lot of bad reasons calculated to appeal to Cesare's dark, vengeful nature.

'If you take a lover, I'll kill you. Try that for size,' Cesare whispered silkily in her ear as he bent over her. 'Much wiser simply to deny you the possibility of temptation, don't you think? Now you won't be tempted to stray and I won't be tempted to commit a crime of passion.'

She stared blindly at the beautifully set candlelit dinner-table and sank down slowly into the seat pulled out for her. 'If you take a lover, I'll kill you.' How on earth on their wedding-day could Cesare even be thinking of her taking a lover? It was so preposterous that he could even imagine that she might be unfaithful that she simply sat there in bemused silence, wondering which one of them was going mad.

CHAPTER SEVEN

PAOLO shook out her napkin and placed it on her lap with a flourish. He uncorked another bottle of champagne, filled their glasses and stood back to proffer a short speech in Italian.

'In case you're interested, Paolo was advancing the fervent good wishes and blessings of our staff and forecasting the tasteful hope that our union will be fruitful and bring children to the household again. He will no doubt be delighted when he realises we were one up in that department even *before* the wedding!'

Mina reddened fiercely. 'Cesare...I don't know where you got the idea that I might——'

'Stray into another bed unless I chained you by force and circumstance to mine?' Cesare drawled, scanning her pink cheeks with derision. 'I've seen you in action, *cara*. I've watched you with Edwin Haland and with Clayton. It was educational. You may be little but you're lethal! If I were an Arab, I'd lock you up in a harem and throw away the key.'

'I have never slept with another man.' Mina lifted her head high. 'You don't deserve that I should tell you that——'

Glittering golden eyes cut her off mid-speech. 'No...I deserve the truth. Clayton was your lover.'

'Steve has never been my lover!' Mina argued, her voice rising sharply.

'I turn my back on you for forty-eight hours,' Cesare murmured in a tone that made the blood in her veins chill, 'and what happens? I find you with Clayton, letting him *touch* you...'

Mina recalled the scene which Cesare had interrupted that day at the garden centre and stared back at him, shattered by how much he could conceal from her. At the time he hadn't batted a single magnificent eyelash, hadn't made the smallest reference to the incident and she had assumed that he had accepted that what he had seen had been entirely innocent, if indeed he even cared enough to consider the matter!

He had been so aloof that day, so utterly set on discussing only Susie... and yet all the time behind that cool front of detachment had lurked this dark, brooding rage... Mina shivered, violently disconcerted by the discovery that Cesare had contrived to hide those feelings from her.

'But then you were childhood sweethearts and familiarity breeds...more familiarity. Obviously you've been playing games with him for years but he still worships the ground you walk on,' Cesare continued with a look of raw contempt. 'Such unquestioning adoration must be hard to live without... but live without it, and him, you shall.'

'Who told you that Steve and I were childhood sweethearts?' Mina prompted shakily.

'Your twin... you will scarcely accuse her of lying?'

'I'm not denying that Steve and I dated in our teens but there's been nothing between us for years——'

'He's in love with you,' Cesare interposed drily.

'He is not in love with me! He *was*... right? But he isn't any more!' Mina argued tautly and with steadily growing anger and frustration. 'As for Winona, she always wanted me to marry Steve so that we could all be one big happy family, and Winona is very persistent, but don't you think that if I had ever wanted Steve I would have married him when he asked me?'

'He hadn't enough to offer. He's never likely to be rich. But he feeds your ego, believes you innocent of every charge, and devotion of that magnitude is rare. I suppose he thinks I got you drunk and wickedly seduced you the night Susie was conceived... you would have settled for him if I hadn't come back.'

Mina threw her napkin aside and stood up, trembling with anger. 'I wish to heaven I had!' she slung unsteadily. 'Steve may never be rich but he knows me far better than you ever will!'

'You will sit down and you will finish your meal,' Cesare told her with flat menace.

'I'm not sharing this table with you!' Mina hissed. 'Not only are you suspicious of my every motive and action, you're *unhinged*, and if you think for one moment that I intend to——'

'*Sit down!*' Cesare said again.

She heard the sound of the door opening and settled back, frustrated by her own reluctance to make a scene in front of the staff. As the first course was removed and the second delivered, she quivered with a combustible mix of anger, bitterness and a sharp, painful sense of self-loathing that she had been foolish enough to imagine that Cesare might have been willing to set the past behind them even briefly.

'I entered this marriage in good faith,' she murmured tautly when they were alone again.

'For Susie's benefit,' Cesare reminded her in a predatory purr. 'And the country life is so good for young children. Fresh air, space to play, not to mention the security that will be provided by the full-time attention of her mother.'

'No matter where we lived Susie would have been assured of that attention.' Mina wouldn't look at him. Pale as paper, she picked up her knife and fork. Although her appetite had vanished, she was determined not to betray the fact. 'But it's obvious to me that no matter what I do you won't trust me.'

'Trust has to be earned and if you don't try to earn it you'll still be sitting here this time next year as trapped as a ship inside a bottle,' Cesare informed her with a deeply sardonic smile as she gazed back at him wide-eyed. 'When you have freely admitted to me that you were guilty of insider trading and satisfied me as to what you did with the money——'

'I didn't do it!' Mina practically screeched at him.

Cesare didn't so much as stop to draw breath. 'And gone at least nine months without the potent effect of another man panting like a rabid dog at your dainty little heels . . . then you might get one escorted trip to London and some of *my* money to spend——'

'Keep your lousy money!' Mina spat in outrage.

Cesare slung her a glittering smile of hard amusement. 'I intend to. I'm going to be the stingiest bastard of your most terrifying nightmares. I'm not issuing you with any credit cards. I'm not giving you any jewellery you could sell. That ring on your finger may look like platinum but it's silver . . .'

With a shaking hand and in a gust of tempestuous fury, Mina wrenched the ring off and flung it down the table at him. It bounced and fell on the floor, unnoticed by either of them. 'Keep that too, you cheapskate!' she launched at him, plunged into deep mortification by the assurance.

'In short I don't believe you'll be leaving this valley under your own steam for quite some time,' Cesare murmured with unhidden satisfaction. 'You can devote all your many talents to being my wife and I can rejoice in the sure knowledge that when I leave you you will be exactly where I left you when I return. Believe it or not *that* is a sensation of security which some men actually take for granted!'

Paolo entered with the dessert course. Mina wanted to snatch it out of his reverent hands and throw it over Cesare. It took immense restraint to control the urge. The atmosphere shimmered around her as she fought to conceal her spitting fury until the older man departed again.

'All I have to do,' she spelt out tremulously, 'is phone my sister——'

'Your sister cringes behind pot plants every time I walk into a room. *Dio mio* . . . I feel terrified!'

'Winona won't let Susie go to anyone but me and no way is Susie coming out here!' Mina swore wildly, desperate to find a weapon to fight back with.

'She'll hand Susie over to her father . . . your brother-in-law will see to that,' Cesare told her.

It had been a foolish threat. Mina bent her head. She did not want to involve her family. She had her pride. Nor did she want to risk upsetting Susie. Her daughter was already very attached to Cesare. Like any young child she had responded to genuine interest and attention and the further knowledge that like her cousins she now had a man she could call Daddy had been all that was required to entrench Cesare firmly in his daughter's affections.

'For better or for worse,' Cesare reminded her softly. 'Although perhaps the line about for richer and for poorer has more relevance to your present air of anguish.'

'What I am feeling right now is *not* anguish, it's rage and a deep, overwhelming desire to push you off the edge of the nearest cliff!' Mina launched back at him wrathfully as she plunged upright, bracing both hands on the edge of the polished table. 'You have just made the biggest miscalculation of your life, Cesare Falcone!'

'You thought I would be fool enough to marry you and leave you free in the heart of London to do whatever you liked? You think I'm stupid or something, *cara*?' A winged ebony brow elevated in sardonic enquiry.

Her teeth clenched together. 'You never once mentioned Steve or that wretched money in recent weeks!'

'Of course not,' Cesare purred, cradling his champagne. 'I don't mind admitting now that restraining myself was a constant challenge but it got you to the altar, didn't it? Now I have exactly what I want. I have my daughter—a legal right to my daughter. But equally importantly I also have you——'

'You do not have me!' Mina snapped like a cat ready to spring, infuriated by his assurance.

Cesare let his golden eyes travel over her and linger on the swell of her heaving breasts. 'I have you,' he repeated. 'Right where I always wanted you. Totally and absolutely dependent——'

'How dare you?' Mina was so enraged by that smouldering explicit look, she could hardly get the words out.

'Maybe not barefoot, pregnant and in the kitchen yet,' Cesare told her lazily, his sensual mouth slanting with raw amusement. 'But give me time.'

Mina lifted a trembling hand and shook it at him. 'If you try to lay one finger on me, I'll make you sorry you were ever born!'

'Our first argument and the ink is scarcely dry on our marriage licence.' Cesare laughed softly and surveyed her from beneath dense black lashes. 'A prudent man would hasten to repair the damage on his wedding night . . . but I've never been prudent. In fact the challenge lends a certain sizzle to my anticipation. I'm willing to bet you a thousand pounds that you share a bed with me tonight.'

'Make it a million for all I care . . . you'll still lose!' Mina flung at him, and walked out of the room, passing by a rather startled Paolo carrying a tray of coffee.

Mina had never been so screamingly angry in her entire life. Another five minutes in Cesare's company and she would have started throwing china. What had originally attracted her to Cesare Falcone now loomed as his most serious flaw! He was unpredictable. As she mounted the stairs, she found several more glaring faults to dwell on.

He was secretive. He had the tenacity of a Rottweiler, the obstinacy of a mule. He could not even imagine that he could possibly be wrong about anything. He was downright sneaky. He plotted and planned as if the blood of the Borgias ran in his rotten veins! And yet he still couldn't see the lousy wood for the trees!

Mina was noisily engaged in hauling the drawers out of a very large chest when her maid entered uncertainly, her knock having gone unanswered. Her dark eyes wide with curiosity, Giulia stared. 'You would like the help, *signora*?'

'No, thank you.' Scarlet at the interruption and breathless, Mina straightened and hitched her gown which had slid down while she was making a futile effort to shift the chest with the drawers still intact. 'I don't need any help,' she lied.

Giulia backed out again with reluctance. Mina hefted out the last drawer and put her shoulder to the chest again, furious that there hadn't been a key in the lock on the door. The massive piece of furniture groaned and shifted a few inches. With a strength born of raging determination, Mina kept on pushing, and when she finally got it across the door she flopped damply to the carpet until it occurred to her that it wouldn't be much of a barrier without the drawers to weight it down again. She was gasping for oxygen by the time she had replaced the drawers and hauled the large sofa below one window over as well.

That achieved, she flopped back on the bed, totally wiped out by all that physical effort. She released the zip on her gown, shimmied it down over her hips and, after another minute or two, peeled off the stockings and the flimsy satin suspender belt. She had never worn either before, she reflected with a kind of mortified fury. Had Cesare gone shopping on her behalf or his? Cesare would like that sort of stuff, she decided bitterly. She ripped off the cobweb-fine panties in rebellion. From now on she would put nothing on her back that she hadn't brought to Sicily and she seriously hoped it did embarrass him!

As she lay there letting the air cool her overheated skin, the anger began to give way to the pain. Cesare had not budged one inch from his conviction that she was a confidence trickster... only he did seem surprisingly keen to hear her admit her wrongdoing out loud all of a sudden. Was it possible that he was having doubts about her guilt?

She suppressed that unlikely hope. Tonight she had dined with a man on a victory roll of sheer, primitive triumph. Control was all-important to Cesare and he now felt one hundred per cent in control of events between them. True, he had had to lure her out to a foreign country and plan to keep her in penury and isolation like some medieval tyrant set on hanging on to an unwilling bride, but there was method in his madness.

A gold-digger would have sweated blood and gone barking mad at his threats but Mina had struggled for so long simply to feed and clothe herself and Susie, she was untouched by them. What would she need money for? She had no bills to pay, and since Cesare had never had to worry about bills he could not possibly realise what a relief it was to be released from that burden.

As for what he had said about Steve... Mina groaned. Steve had avoided her like the plague from the instant he'd learnt that she was getting married to Cesare. In a weak moment, Mina had awkwardly asked her twin how Steve had taken the news.

'How do you think?' Winona had muttered with an air of helpless condemnation. 'He was shattered. He thought you hated Cesare.'

And somehow the ball of guilt had been landed right back into Mina's court. Yet what had she done? At twenty she had told Steve that she didn't love him enough to marry him, and in recent years she had honestly believed that he had moved on from her, learned to accept her as a friend and nothing more. But the instant Cesare had physically entered the picture again Steve had gone haywire, behaving as though Cesare were some rival who had supplanted him when he was well aware that she hadn't even met Cesare when they'd broken up. Men! Who needs them? Mina thought miserably.

What hurt the most was Cesare's belief that she was capable of flitting from his bed into Steve's. It was a savage irony that she had never been very attracted to Steve. She had liked him, laughed with him and enjoyed his company but the day Steve not unnaturally demanded a little more intimacy from the girl he loved had been the same day that Mina had finally accepted that she didn't love him in the same way that he loved her. If it hadn't been for Roger and Winona, her relationship with Steve would have died years sooner than it actually had. The pressure to make the happy twosome into an even happier foursome had been intense.

How could Cesare even think that she had casually shared those same intimacies with another man? Making love was so...so intensely personal. Or at least it had been on Mina's side. But then she loved Cesare. He did not love her. Love made a difference, she decided wretchedly. What was special to her was not that special to him. Presumably, he had not been celibate for the past four years. As soon as that thought occurred to her she buried it again because it hurt terribly to think of him in another woman's arms, and after what he had done to her tonight that vulnerability made her loathe herself.

Face it, she told herself painfully, in Cesare's eyes, you're a tramp. Why? He got you into bed the first time he kissed you, came back four years later, and within twenty-four hours, in spite of every insult, threat and accusation, you succumbed a second time. No wonder he thinks you're easy; no wonder he doesn't respect you; no wonder he seems to think you're the next best thing to a raving nymphomaniac.

Hadn't she behaved like one? Admittedly she had been a late starter at twenty-two, but Cesare appeared to believe that one night with him had turned her into a man-eater, which was painfully ironic when he was the only man alive who brought out that wanton side of her nature. Shamefacedly, Mina surveyed the barricaded door. Was it to keep him out or to prevent her from surrendering to temptation?

A sound that she instinctively recognised as that of a door opening jerked her head round in search of the source of such an impossibility. She flew up into a sitting position, her heartbeat racing madly as she incredulously surveyed a section of the dark wall-panelling swinging out.

For a split-second she was frozen until she recalled her own nudity. In horror, a stifled gasp of sheer fright escaping her, she grabbed frantically at the silky spread beneath her, clawing the folds up and over her as best she could. 'Dear God . . .' she began weakly.

Cesare appeared in the dark mouth of a doorway which she had not even suspected existed. Clad only in a short black silk robe, he stood there for a timeless moment, undeniably enthralled by the picture Mina made, her golden hair tumbling round her hectically flushed face, violet eyes gleaming as bright as jewels, her slender body scantily wrapped in the rainbow hues of the bedspread.

Colliding with that smouldering golden gaze, Mina went rigid. 'You rat!' she suddenly exploded. 'There was a secret door!'

'A secret what?' Cesare breathed, ebony brows drawing together as he frowned at her with what she considered to be a spurious air of incomprehension.

'Nothing like hedging your bets!' Mina condemned furiously, fit to be tied at having being surprised in such a situation, curled up on the bed stark naked behind a ridiculously barricaded door when all the time all he had had to do was walk through another door!

'What are you talking about?' With visible difficulty, Cesare trailed his hot gaze from her and closed the door behind him. 'A *secret* door?' he queried, his hand lingering for an expressive moment on the wooden handle which a closer scrutiny of the panelled wall would have revealed. 'What is secret about it? It links our bedrooms.'

'I don't want a link between our bedrooms!' Mina shot at him angrily. 'Get out!'

But Cesare's attention had strayed, not surprisingly, to the furniture blocking the other entrance to the bedroom. For a full five seconds he simply stared and then he threw back his dark head and roared with laughter. 'You put up barricades?' he questioned with incredulous amusement.

Mina froze into a small graven image as unamused as Queen Victoria might have been but her cheeks burned hotter than ever. Never in her life had she felt more ridiculous.

'And such large barricades,' Cesare remarked in a strained voice, flicking the massive chest of drawers a deeply appreciative glance before looking back at her with mocking respect at her achievement. 'And all that considerable effort wasted, it would seem... I do hope you haven't exhausted yourself.'

Mina unfroze and clawed up more of the bedspread. 'Get out of here, Cesare!'

'But this is our wedding night, *cara*.'

Mina's teeth clenched. She wanted to leap off the bed and thump him but she was afraid that the bedspread would fall off. 'The answer is *no*!'

A winged ebony brow elevated. 'Did I ask a question?'

'You need it spelt out to you?' Mina intoned, quivering with fury. 'OK. I am not prepared to share a bed with a man who thinks I'm a gold-digging, dishonest tramp!'

'Why not?' Cesare enquired softly. 'If I'm prepared to sacrifice my principles——'

'*Yours*?' Mina flared in disbelief.

'Who else's? If I could keep my hands off you, don't you think I would?' Cesare murmured with grim satire. 'Do you really think that it was my secret ambition to take a wife who *could* be described as a gold-digging, dishonest tramp?'

'How dare you?' Mina spat.

'You brought the subject up first, and, if you want the reality to extend to the bedroom, so be it,' Cesare decreed with ruthless bite, a hard, purposeful twist to his expressive mouth. 'But know it now and accept it—you are going to change. Sooner or later you will tire of hiding behind your pathetic lies and you will tell the truth about what you did four years ago——'

'I didn't bloody well *do* anything!' Mina screamed at him in a tempestuous surge of fury. 'And if you fondly imagine that I'm going to hang my head in shame over something I didn't do——'

'No remorse . . . no forgiveness.' Brilliant golden eyes rested on her with incipient threat. 'Don't say you weren't warned.'

'You are out of your mind,' Mina whispered, helplessly intimidated. 'I did nothing——'

'You betrayed my trust,' Cesare condemned, a dark anger shimmering suddenly into the heavy atmosphere. 'You betrayed me.'

And nothing else mattered, she registered, a sudden chill enclosing her flesh.

'And you did it with such panache. You told me you loved me,' Cesare murmured in a tone so quiet that goose-bumps prickled over her exposed skin.

Mina had turned very pale. Painful chagrin was surging through her in waves. She did not want to be reminded of how naïve she had been then, swept off to bed one night and spilling out her heart like an infatuated adolescent who lacked all adult reserve.

'And I actually believed you,' Cesare completed with sudden rawness.

'No doubt it gave you quite a kick,' Mina condemned jerkily.

'Not half as much of a kick as keeping you here for my personal entertainment will give me.' In one unhurried movement, Cesare loosened the tie at his lean waist and shed the robe.

Mina took one staggered glance at the savage potency of his powerful sun-darkened physique and something clenched hard deep in the pit of her stomach, her skin dampening in a tide of treacherous awareness so strong that it left her weak and trembling.

She squeezed her eyes shut in rebellion, frantically fighting the raw sexual charge fingering flames of dangerous fire into an already combustible atmosphere. She would not allow him to do this to her again, she swore to herself. She would control this madness which took no account of anything but the physical, which wiped out every thought and deed. She owed that to herself.

The bed gave slightly with his weight. Mina mentally braced herself for his first touch but it didn't come. The silence rushed and surged around her with suffocating intensity. When she couldn't stand the suspense any longer, her lashes lifted.

Cesare was lying in a careless sprawl beside her, looking up at her with eyes of shimmering gold that burned. Her breath shortened in her throat.

'You know why I gave you that job?' he murmured conversationally. 'You were the best candidate and I made a conscious effort not to be sexist. I told myself that the fact that I found you attractive should not interfere with my assessment of your abilities. It was, in short *my* problem . . . but within days I sensed that my problem was developing into *our* problem. You wanted me too——'

'Not that soon . . . no, I didn't!' she protested.

Cesare lifted an indolent brown hand and pressed a forefinger against her strained mouth in reproof as she automatically bent over him. 'And you couldn't hide it. On that level I could read you like a billboard.'

Her lips moved tremulously against his finger, a tiny little quiver of unbelievable tension shrilling through every nerve-ending. '*No* . . .'

'But I fought the good fight of restraint on your behalf. I was a complete gentleman.' A bitter curve slanted his hard mouth as he gazed up at her, electrifying golden eyes sentencing her to stillness. 'No way was I going to take you abroad with me—too many late nights...too much intimacy...'

'Too many other women,' Mina filled in tightly.

'Diversions which failed.'

'You wanted me to resign,' she whispered.

'You were distracting me.' Cesare rubbed his fingertip gently across the soft fullness of her lower lip. 'I had incredible fantasies about you. Long before I ever touched you, I had had you a thousand times in my dreams.'

Her breath hung suspended, her cheeks hotly flushed, but she couldn't tear her mesmerised gaze from his because he was giving her a glimpse of another world, *his* world, but it was an infinitely more physical one than hers had been. A spasm of pain pierced her. He talked about sex, nothing else...but then Cesare was one very sexy man.

'Restraint started out exciting and became deeply painful,' he muttered with feeling. 'You bent over a desk and showed me a mere inch of thigh and I burned and I ached like a teenager craving his first score...any time, any place—it didn't matter. The longer you stayed, the deeper I got in, the harder I had to fight, until it got to the stage where you were the only thing on my mind. It pushed me to the edge... That last week, your time was up...'

Entirely focused on him, she felt light-headed. 'I didn't know——'

'Didn't know what?' Cesare whispered unevenly, dropping his hand to the bedspread wrapped beneath her arms as he coiled fluidly up so that their eyes locked. 'That wanting like that is rare? That most people go all their lives without ever feeling like this? It's a hunger so strong it has to be satisfied . . . and it's bound to rage out of control.'

She recognised an incredibly sensitised awareness of her every sense. A deep languor enclosed her limbs. Silence like a pulsebeat thundered in her eardrums. Without even understanding how it had happened, she was pitched on an electrifying high of anticipation. Reason attempted to stir in the darkness of her mind as she collided dry-mouthed with eyes of molten gold but reason wasn't powerful enough to still the mad race of her pulses or the accelerated thump of her heart as her breasts swelled and her nipples stiffened into tight little buds.

Lean fingers loosened the silken barrier, tugged it slowly down. Her breath rattled in her throat, stirring her breasts as he bared them. The knowledge that he couldn't take his eyes off her was terrifyingly exciting. His strong face was dark, intent as he closed his hands round her forearms, pulled her down on top of him and almost simultaneously bent her back, engulfing a pouting pink nipple with the hungry heat of his mouth.

She gasped under the shock wave of sensation that tore through every nerve-ending, her fingers biting into a broad shoulder, then spearing into the dark depths of his hair, and the thought that this was not supposed to be happening came to her again. She squeezed her eyes tightly shut, a sob locking her vocal cords. Never in all her life had she ever wanted anything as badly as she wanted him at that moment. Her body greedily craved the passion but her heart craved the physical closeness, the freedom to touch, to express in silence the need and love she dared not express in words. It was like being torn in two...

One hand anchoring into her tumbling silky hair, he brought her head up. 'Four years ago I told myself it was only chemistry, only an accidental explosion, but no other woman makes me feel like this,' he breathed raggedly.

'But you don't——' And all that she could not bring herself to say darkened her anguished eyes. You don't love me, you don't like me, you don't respect me. And the awareness that she would have settled for any one of the three tortured her. 'There has to be more,' she muttered shakily. 'For me, there has to be more...'

His hand moved expertly against her breast, making her tauten and jerk, live-wire sensation turning her very bones to melting honey. 'You'll have to do what I do...settle for what you *can* have; forget about the rest,' he delivered harshly.

'But I want——'

'This... this is what you want!' Without warning, he took her mouth in a raw surge of dominating passion and the world blacked out, plunging her into the hot darkness beckoning behind her lowered eyelids.

His tongue plunged between her lips, seeking out the tender interior beyond, and she trembled violently as he forced her closer, deftly parting her thighs so that she knelt astride him. A gasp of shock escaped her at the sudden crashing intimacy of her position and she stiffened but, with an unashamed groan of intense satisfaction, Cesare prevented her retreat, powerful hands curving to the swell of her hips as he ravished her mouth with an urgent hunger then ripped away the last lingering remnant of her control.

With one kiss, he made her burn hotter than hellfire. It was like being consumed. Her swollen breasts were crushed against him, the hair roughening his broad chest abrading her sensitive nipples. Every part of her was connected to the hot, hard heat of him, and when he moved, letting her feel the thrusting readiness of his manhood against the very heart of her, she moaned with excitement, so far beyond control that he was the only stable entity she could cling to.

'*This* is what we have,' Cesare muttered thickly, holding her steady with long fingers knotted into her hair, tugging her head back so that he could look at her face. 'Don't tell me it's not enough. *Dio* ... three weeks without touching you! I punish you, I punish myself. Does that please you?'

'No...' she mumbled, drowning in his smouldering golden eyes.

He leant over her, nibbled erotically at the reddened fullness of her lower lip, and as she trembled, he uttered a strangled groan and shuddered, every muscle tautening with whipcord tension as he lifted her against him, searching out the moist heat between her thighs. She writhed, cried out, unbearable sensation rising to a sudden shattering peak that was pure torment.

'I can't wait.' He brought her down to him with aching slowness and agonising control, forging his entry little by little, and it was so staggeringly exciting that she somehow wanted to faint with delight and scream with frustration at the same time. She closed her eyes, instinctively attempting to conceal the wildness of her own desperate hunger.

'Look at me,' Cesare demanded, stilling.

'Don't stop!' she gasped between clenched teeth.

'Open your eyes,' he grated. Her lashes flew up, revealing her puzzlement.

'I want to watch you...I want to be sure you know it's me inside you,' he rasped with sizzling bite, his lean features taut with intense sexual arousal and equally intense determination.

She was far beyond reasoning. Quivering with out-of-control response to what he was making her feel, she looked blankly back at him. 'Cesare...?'

'*Sì*...Cesare...nobody else...ever again,' he spelt out between gritted teeth, perspiration dampening his golden skin. And with riveting abruptness he withdrew from her and flipped her backwards across the tumbled bedspread, coming down on top of her in one fluid movement, pinning her startled hands to the mattress and thrusting into her yielding flesh with driving force. Later she would remember it as the most intensely erotic shock he had ever given her. She was stunned and then stunned again by a wave of sheer blinding excitement.

He took her by storm and she felt possessed, driven, inflamed by the feeling that he was out of control. All honeyed pliancy and complicity, every fibre of her body pitched to an unbelievable height of anticipation, she let herself go, lost herself entirely in the thunder of her own crazed heartbeat and the fevered tension coiling ever tighter inside her. With every driving thrust he took her higher, and then suddenly the whole world went multi-coloured, her back arching, her teeth clenching as she sobbed, 'I love you... I love you!' on the peak of a shuddering and ecstatic wave of drowning pleasure.

Clawing back up through the layers of indolent languor which enclosed her, Mina noticed the silence first. It vibrated. Cesare freed himself from the tangle of their damp limbs and slid on to his side, releasing her from his weight, letting cooler air wash over her hot skin.

'Don't feed me bull like that again,' he murmured with lancing derision.

With an uncertain hand she reached for the bedspread but it was too tangled to offer her any speedy hope of a covering. Hearing that tone from him in the aftermath of his passion was like having a knife plunged into her heart. It made her want to curl up and die. It negated the pleasure and, worse, it made her wanton craving of that same pleasure seem a shameful and weak self-betrayal.

'What are you talking about?' she muttered, because she really didn't know.

'Hearing you tell me that you love me has to be the biggest turn-off I know,' Cesare imparted with chilling emphasis.

She turned away from him, gripped by sudden com-prehension, slaughtered by rejection. Only now did she recall what she had said at that blinding instant of climax when her body and her mind had been in passion's grip.

'But then maybe you said it out of habit,' Cesare suggested with contempt.

'Habit?' she queried tremulously, astounded to hear her own voice.

'Maybe Clayton likes the illusion...I don't. I don't have any illusions left about you and when you don't have expectations you don't get disappointed,' he asserted with a harsh laugh. 'And he must have been very disappointed today when he finally had to face that your "love" goes to the highest bidder!'

Mina understood then and her stomach heaved. Her hands clenched, her fingernails scoring sharp crescents into the soft skin of her palms. Then, without any warning at all, the anger came, surging up out of the devastating pain of her emotions and taking over...

CHAPTER EIGHT

IN ONE wrathful movement Mina sat up, her delicate facial bones stiff, her amethyst eyes brilliant with rage. 'I've had enough of this... I won't listen to one more filthy insinuation!' she told him furiously. 'Maybe you'd like to tell me how Steve and I could possibly have carried on some sleazy affair with Roger and Winona looking on? You're talking about four people who have known each other all their lives—and if you sneeze Winona notices!'

Cesare had tautened in astonishment, deep-set dark eyes fixed intently to her. His sensual mouth took on an unexpected quirk of amusement. 'I can believe *that*——'

But not the rest of it?' Mina cut in rawly. 'Why do you think Steve hates you so much? Steve and I dated for four years and we were never intimate, never even partially intimate! But I only knew you for three months and he actually dared to tell me once that that was the hardest thing of all for him to accept...and I thought at the time, To hell with fragile male egos—and I *still* think it!'

'Mina——'

'So if you want to go on thinking that I bounced straight out of bed with you into bed with him, go ahead! I'll phone and tell Steve...he would be absolutely delighted to know you think that! But how dare you try to drag me down to the level of a slot on some pathetic male sexual score card?'

A dark flush of blood had highlighted his hard cheekbones. 'That was not what I was doing,' he told her rawly.

'That's exactly what you were doing! All that sophistication on the surface, and underneath what are you?' Mina splintered tempestuously. 'You're so primitive you haven't even made it on to the bottom rung of the evolutionary ladder!'

'Whatever turns you on, *cara*,' Cesare murmured, eyes a sliver of flaring gold below his black lashes.

Mina sucked in oxygen with an audible hiss, outraged by the comeback. 'You're not even listening to me, are you?'

'I'm listening to you telling me what you know I want to believe,' Cesare returned with a sardonic laugh.

That was the last straw. If she tried to defend herself she was immediately suspected of some devious motivation. The anger went out of her, snuffed like a candle. 'Well, that's it, then, isn't it?' she whispered bitterly. 'I'm wasting my breath. Do you have to sleep here or do I get a reward for winning your lousy bet for you?'

'That was a joke——'

'That was an insult.'

The silence thrummed with violent undertones.

'That was an insult,' Cesare finally conceded, startling her with the admission.

'You hate me.' Pain fractured her voice, making her seal her lips and swallow hard.

'Sometimes.' Not troubling to deny the fact, Cesare sprang fluidly off the bed. His vibrant features unusually still, he studied her with dark-as-night eyes and his beautifully shaped mouth hardened. 'But four years ago you could have had it all, *cara*. That's the real joke. You were so busy plotting and planning you couldn't see what was right under your nose. You sold me down the river for a pittance when you could have had so much more.'

'I don't know what you're talking about.' And don't much care, Mina completed inwardly, torn apart by the ever deepening gulf between them. It was a wedding night she would never forget, a humiliation she would never forget, and it seemed to her now that no matter what she did, no matter what she said Cesare would never listen. His prejudices were too entrenched after four years of brooding on what he saw as her betrayal.

'I was in love with you.'

Her lashes fluttered up, revealing dazed violet eyes. 'No...you weren't,' she said jerkily.

'It hit me like a bolt of lightening on the flight to Hong Kong. *My* moment of truth,' he drawled with derision.

Mina had turned white, shock reverberating through her. 'No,' she protested again. 'You weren't in love with me.'

'Madly in love. I was thinking wedding-bells, honeymoons, christenings,' Cesare reeled off with a scornful smile that chilled her.

Mina was paralysed by what he was telling her. It was like being told she had won a fortune and then discovering that she had lost the ticket required to prove her claim. It also ripped asunder her view of the past. For so long she had believed that Cesare had simply used her for a few hours of light entertainment and then regretted it but the picture he drew now devastated her, filled her with an embittered sense of loss and a raging resentment against the injustice which had parted them.

'But not for long,' she whispered unsteadily.

'No, not for long,' Cesare agreed. 'But the subject of your wheeling and dealing on the stock-market is currently closed.'

'It can't be closed. It can never be closed!' she told him in disbelief. 'If you had once given me the opportunity to speak to you without Susie around *before* the wedding, I would have demanded that you produce the evidence that you say you have!'

Cesare dealt her a look of savage derision. 'Meet your partner in crime...'

'I beg your pardon?'

'I destroyed the evidence.'

'You did *what*?' Mina gasped incredulously.

'Think about it,' Cesare advised. 'You're the mother of my child. You're my wife now. To retain documents which could be used against you in criminal proceedings would be utter madness. Suppose that by some accident that evidence fell into the wrong hands? It was a risk I could no longer take. As long as you are my wife, I will protect you.'

She stared at him in shattered silence. Cesare had immense respect for the forces of law and order. That he had actually disposed of the evidence of an apparent fraud shook her rigid. It was not an act which he would have undertaken lightly. Indeed she was convinced it would have gone very much against his natural inclinations. 'Meet your partner in crime', he had said grimly, bitter at the role which he felt had been forced on him. He would protect her because she was Susie's mother.

'But I needed to see that evidence,' Mina told him tensely, a giant surge of frustration currenting through her taut body. 'I wanted to——'

'Make up nonsensical stories to explain every piece of it away?' Cesare derided. 'That's why I wouldn't have shown it to you.'

'So I'm not to be allowed the chance to defend myself——'

'I want no more lies,' Cesare interposed coldly. 'I've heard enough of them. As for the money...on that count I suspect you are telling me the truth. I don't think you have anything left to stash away.'

Mina took a deep breath, 'I didn't do it,' she murmured with taut emphasis. 'You have to give me the chance to prove that.'

His strong face hardened. 'When you talk in this vein, you anger me more. The subject is closed until you are prepared to admit the truth. *Buonanotte, cara.*'

If there had been anything within reach she would have thrown it at him! Balked of even the smallest chance to clear her name, Mina was inflamed by raw resentment. But she had learnt something which she had naïvely failed to grasp until now. Cesare was still determined to make her pay for her supposed crime. He might not have been prepared to report her to the authorities but that was only because he intended to deal out punishment personally.

And he was considerably more ruthless than any judge would have been. She was not to be allowed any form of hearing. Cesare had decided that she was guilty and that was that and now the sentence was being carried out. She was to be marooned in isolation until she showed signs of repentance.

What form of repentance did Cesare envisage? She was to confess and no doubt do a lot of weeping and begging for forgiveness until honour was satisfied. He was really putting on the thumbscrews, she reflected hysterically. No shopping, no nightclubs, no other men... wow! How on earth would she ever survive such deprivations? He even seemed to think that simply being at home with Susie all day would be a punishment, not realising that that was a luxury she was eagerly looking forward to.

But Cesare had also told her that he loved her four years ago... That tore her in two. Yet what kind of love had it been that he had judged her guilty with such immediacy that he had instantly sacked her? He hadn't even been prepared to wait until he returned from Hong Kong. He had not questioned her guilt. Nor had he allowed his feelings to come between him and his sense of right and wrong. It occurred to Mina for the first time that the evidence against her must have been overwhelming.

Right now if she persisted in raising the subject and continually reiterating her innocence it would push them even further apart, and yet how could she remain silent? Someone in Falcone Industries had set her up. She no longer had any doubt of that fact. Cesare had only been in Hong Kong for ten days and on the fifth day she had been sacked.

So who had given Cesare the information which had made her the victim of someone else's fraud? It had all happened so incredibly fast. And finally, where had that fifty thousand pounds gone when it had finally been removed from her account?

She decided to write to her bank but she wondered ruefully if they would even consider divulging such information or if they would retain records of such a transfer this long after the event. Yet surely whoever had accepted back that money had to be the real perpetrator of the crime, or at the very least an accomplice? The ability to prove that that money had left her account again would mean nothing. Cesare would merely assume that she had shifted it somewhere else. But she had to try, didn't she? She had to at least try.

Impulsively she scrambled back out of bed, yanked a nightie out of a drawer, slid into it in a rush and then opened the communicating door. The room beyond was in darkness but for a triangle of light showing from an ajar door at the other end. She could hear a shower running. She switched on the light beside the bed and hovered.

A few minutes later, Cesare emerged towelling his hair dry. He stopped dead, flaring golden eyes shimmering over her slender figure. Suddenly Mina became awesomely conscious both of the flimsy nature of the silk nightdress and the nudity of his lean, golden body.

'Do you ever think of anything else?' she heard herself demand helplessly, her skin burning with awareness at the explicit sensuality of his unashamed appraisal. 'I came in here to talk seriously about something and I only want you to listen.'

He cast aside the towel, shifted a shoulder in an infuriatingly careless shrug. It was not encouraging but Mina was determined to say her piece. She told him about the money which had appeared and then disappeared from her bank account four years previously. His dark features remained maddeningly uninformative. When she came to a breathless halt, he strolled past her and closed the door between their bedrooms.

'Aren't you going to say anything?' she prompted tautly.

'For a story right off the top of your head, it's agile...even clever. It would be very difficult to prove or disprove after this length of time,' Cesare drawled.

Mina linked her hands together tightly and looked levelly back at him. 'I thought that maybe you could help me to check it out.'

'*Madre di Dio*...do I look that gullible?' he raked back at her incredulously.

Wild colour sprang up in her cheeks, her eyes glittering. 'No, you look stupid!' Mina hissed back at him hotly. 'Stupid...stubborn and self-satisfied, and I'm fed up to the back teeth with you!'

Cesare quirked an ebony brow. 'Is that why you drifted in here dressed to kill?'

'Dressed to *what*?' Mina gasped, studying him with splintering amethyst enquiry. 'You'd find a sack an enticement, wouldn't you?'

'On you...probably,' Cesare conceded without skipping a beat as he strolled closer. 'As you said, I'm way down the evolutionary ladder, *cara*.'

'Back off, you conceited jerk! If you think I came in here——'

'To stay? I do think that,' he confirmed, reaching out a lean hand and snapping it round her wrist. '*Dio mio, cara*...do you really think I'll let you walk away in a huff just because I neglected to swallow your entertaining but wholly improbable fairy-tale?'

As he propelled her closer, Mina attempted to free herself from his hold. 'It wasn't a fairy-tale, damn you!'

In a lightning-swift movement he enclosed her other wrist and drew her firmly towards him, a fiercely intent look stamped on his lean features.

'Cesare, let go of me!' Mina panted in a fury, shaken to rediscover that she was absolutely powerless against that effortless strength.

'I want you again.' He lowered his dark head and let the tip of his tongue pierce erotically between her parted lips.

Her knees wobbled, a glow of instantaneous heat igniting treacherously inside her. Involuntarily she opened her mouth for him but he played with her, an expert erotic gamester, enforcing surrender without giving her a tithe of what she helplessly sought. The breath was trapped in her throat as the remorseless heat spread through her, making her tingle and tense, charging every nerve-ending with drowning weakness. He nibbled teasingly at her lower lip and a stifled sound of frustration escaped low in her throat.

'I could make you beg . . .' Cesare whispered thickly. 'But I don't think I have that much control.'

She shivered violently as he settled a powerful hand to the soft swell of her hips and crushed her against him. He was hotly aroused. The thin silk was no barrier against the throbbing heat of him. Her lower limbs turned to water. His hands brushed aside the straps on her shoulders, thrusting them down over her arms while she stood there entrapped by her own wanton susceptibility.

His breath fanning her cheek, he licked along the tremulous line of her reddened lower lip and let his fingers rise to the swelling fullness of her breasts, his thumbs glancing across the pouting tautness of her nipples. A hot damp ache stirred unbearably between her thighs and she swayed, weak in the ruthless grip of the sensations he could evoke. Her body wasn't her own any more. He shifted sinuously against her and then closed his arms round her, lifting her up, and when he kissed her the whole world went into a tailspin and she clutched wildly at his hair, at any part of him she could reach, and kissed him back.

With a guttural groan, he brought her down on the bed, pinioning her beneath him, one hand twisted in her golden hair as he ravished her mouth over and over again until she was dizzy and breathless and utterly bemused by the extent of her own quivering, shameless excitement.

'This time . . . you really are mine,' Cesare murmured roughly, framing her hectically flushed face with hard, possessive hands as he looked down at her, eyes of molten gold alight with desire and primitive satisfaction. But those hands weren't quite steady and that big, powerful body trembled in the circle of her arms. On a very female level, she was fully attuned to that awareness.

'Absolutely mine,' Cesare savoured, lowering his dark head to her breasts, circling a taut bud with the tip of his tongue and then hungrily engulfing her achingly tender flesh with the raw heat of his mouth.

Sensation shot lightning bolts of fire through her and she lifted a hand, clenched it fiercely into the smooth skin of his shoulder. He rolled on to his side, taking her with him, and kissed her again, hotly, invasively, triumphantly, making every sense sing wildly. Desperate to touch him, she splayed her fingers against the hard wall of his chest, feeling the pull of his muscles as he tensed, instinctively following the arrowing dark furrow of hair and then hesitating fatally, passion pierced by sudden recall of her own ignorance.

'Don't stop now,' Cesare groaned, his teeth nipping at the extended line of her throat, making her jerk and twist and then still in shock as he told her raggedly exactly what he wanted and carried her hand down over the fiercely contacted muscles of his taut stomach to the thrusting power of his arousal.

In the lamplight her eyes flew wide, hectic pink firing her cheeks. 'I—I——'

Gazing down at her with a look of wonderment, Cesare suddenly threw back his dark head and loosed a husky laugh of amused understanding. 'No, we didn't do that before.' He murmured something soft in Italian, raking her with slumbrous eyes as he eased her back to him. 'So sometimes you *do* tell the truth, *cara...*'

Before she could regain the power of speech, he devoured her mouth with compelling urgency, enforcing the response that he had already learned was his to call up at will. He pushed her back against the pillows with unexpected gentleness. Reason drifted away again as though he had slammed a door shut. He ran his tongue in a glancing foray down the valley between her breasts, employing his caressing hands with devastating effect as he slid down her quivering body.

And long before she had even guessed his intention he had engaged her in something so impossibly intimate that she tautened in instinctive rejection, only to gasp and grit her teeth and find control flying out of reach within seconds. The intensity of pleasure overwhelmed her. The tormenting ache inside her expanded, the pressure built and intensified and she sobbed, raking her nails down the sheet beneath her, her hips rising in a feverish supplication as old as time. Wild need screamed through every torturously sensitised inch of her.

'Cesare...' she gasped helplessly on the peak of a hunger too painful to be borne.

'*Bella mia....*' With a savage groan, he plunged into her, and the wildness of pure sensation took over as he surged inside her in a driving possession, moving harder and faster with a shuddering intensity that utterly controlled. Remorselessly he took her with him to the heights of mind-blowing ecstasy. When release came in a flood of shattering sensation, it felt like flying into the sun and burning up...

Mina wakened with a frantic start when the door opened. She snatched the sheet up over her in sleepy consternation as Giulia appeared with a laden tray. '*Buongiorno, signora.*'

'*Buongiorno*,' she mumbled, stealing a glance round the unfamiliar room and the mortifyingly tossed bed. Cesare's room... Cesare's bed.

Giulia pulled back the curtains letting the sunlight flood in. 'You want I run bath, *signora*?'

'No, thanks.' Even to her own ears Mina sounded a little shrill. Having staff around added a whole new dimension to embarrassment, she decided.

Wild imagery of the night before choked her on her first sip of fruit juice. It was little wonder she had slept so late. Hot pink drenched her skin as she noticed a tiny bluish bruise on one breast and became aware of the unaccustomed ache which was doubtless the reward of an orgy of lovemaking. Don't kid yourself, she urged herself painfully. You were making love, he was having sex...

She had come into this bedroom simply to talk yet talking had bitten the dust ludicrously fast. It was all very well to complain that Cesare did not take her seriously but succumbing to his every lustful advance with mindless, breathless surrender was not exactly the intelligent approach likely to impress a rich, arrogant Sicilian tycoon. The bedroom was a battlefield with a man of Cesare Falcone's ilk. Every time she went weak at the knees in his radius she was letting herself down!

When he had told her that he had been in love with her four years ago, all sorts of softened feelings had foolishly blossomed inside her. But loving Cesare did not mean she didn't see his flaws. She could well imagine him getting half way to Hong Kong before it dawned on him that he might actually be in love. Having satiated himself with sex, she thought darkly, there had then been space for him to consider feelings.

But in five long days he had made no attempt to contact her. There had been no phone calls. Indeed phones which had normally rung off the hook in her office while he was away had remained defiantly silent. It was as if the world had stopped dead and on the fifth evening she had gone home to that special delivery. Dismissal and rejection combined.

Pain engulfed her. He might think he had loved her but Mina didn't believe that what he had been feeling then was love. He had openly admitted that he had wanted her physically from the very first moment he saw her. And for three months he had fought that desire. Shamelessly candid on the subject, he had even admitted seeing other women in an attempt to satisfy that lust elsewhere.

But when that hadn't worked he had decided to take her to bed. Neither of them had been able to ignore, suppress or control that powerful attraction and Mina was painfully convinced that what Cesare had briefly interpreted as love had merely been a fancy word for intense sexual desire. No doubt had fate allowed him more time with her, he would have got bored and appreciated that reality.

The door opened. Her hand shook so badly when she saw him that she had to put her cup of coffee back down on the tray. He strolled to the foot of the bed and smiled with raw brilliance. And that was it. He didn't even need to open his mouth. She wanted to throw the tray at him.

'I took down the barricades next door,' he drawled indolently.

Mina turned a beetroot colour and reached back for her coffee, any excuse to avoid looking at him again. But it really didn't matter. He was etched in her mind's eye anyway. Drop-dead gorgeous in faded tight jeans which clung to narrow hips and long, lean thighs, and a casual white polo shirt which hugged broad shoulders and a superbly muscular chest. He looked stunningly handsome... and one hundred per cent predator on the prowl.

'You look spectacular,' he murmured, his accent growling sexily along every syllable of the extraordinary assurance.

'Spectacular'—with her hair on end, last night's make-up probably blackening her eyes and teeth-marks in impossibly intimate places? Inwardly she cringed from her own weakness. There were degrees of susceptibility. Consummating their marriage was one thing. Throwing herself heart and soul into an orgy was another thing entirely.

She stole an upward glance and collided with another slow burning smile that was intimately redolent of the erotic memories tormenting her. Only it was obvious that Cesare was not being tormented. He was quite visibly on a high. If he had brought out a bottle of champagne and uncorked it, she wouldn't have been surprised.

'Why are you smiling all of a sudden?' Mina muttered suspiciously.

'You want an honest answer?'

'Last night about the only thing you didn't threaten me with was a dungeon and chains!'

'Celibacy doesn't agree with me.' Deep-set dark eyes rested on her with unconcealed satisfaction.

Mina lost her heady colour and gulped back cooling coffee in an effort to conceal how devastating she found that response. They were married and she didn't feel married. She squinted at her bare finger, dimly recalled hurling the ring down the table down at him. She had no desire to go looking for that ring. It was the empty symbol of a relationship which did not exist on his side of the fence.

Cesare's prime motivation had been acquiring his daughter. Since he had been quite honest about that from the outset, why had she married him still cherishing such naïve expectations? Shouldn't his behaviour before the wedding have been a sufficient warning of what lay ahead? Agonising as it was to face hard reality, she made herself face it. Cesare had only one use for her and it was a pretty basic one.

Weeks ago in London, he had said he would pay the price for her sexual favours and in the end the price had turned out to be marriage. Her skin chilled at that acknowledgement. He might not have wanted to marry her but right now Cesare thought he had it all. He had Susie, he had a convenient mother for Susie and he had an outlet for that shockingly high-powered sex drive of his. Little wonder that he was content with the current status quo. It demanded nothing from him.

She had less value than a mistress, none at all as a wife. Now that he had her stashed in the darkest depths of Sicily, he didn't give a damn about her feelings or her needs. Why should he? He thought she was a money-grubbing confidence trickster finally receiving her just deserts. No pain, no gain. That was the level on which that brooding Latin temperament of his functioned and in sharing a bed with him she betrayed her self-respect.

'I also accept that you weren't lying about Clayton,' Cesare imparted lazily, as though he was merely mentioning it in an afterthought, golden eyes resting on her with unashamed gratification. 'Whatever game you were playing with him, you weren't sleeping with him.'

Flames of angry colour drenched her cheeks. So he finally believed her about something. But it was a case of too little too late. Indeed when she registered just how primitively pleased Cesare was by the knowledge that he had been her only lover, ironically she found herself wishing that she had kept her mouth shut.

He harboured a medieval streak of outright sexual possessiveness. She should have left him to stew in the pit of his own dark suspicions. He hadn't deserved the truth but Mina's essential honesty had betrayed her. Foolishly she had fallen in to the thankless habit of constantly defending herself, vainly struggling to establish a relationship which had a future with the man she loved…and where had it got her? she asked herself now.

'How would you like to spend the day?' he enquired, magnificently untouched by the bitter regrets attacking her.

'Dressing in sackcloth and ashes and jumping off a cliff.'

'That is not funny.'

'I don't feel funny...I feel...' Her voice wobbled. 'I feel used and angry and very, very bitter!'

In despair, she thrust away the tray, slid out of bed and returned to her own room, for once indifferent to her own lack of clothing.

'Mina...?'

'Look, leave me alone!' she slung back at him shakily, and vanished into the bathroom.

Well, her generosity had finally died, she told herself. Loving him didn't mean she had to make a doormat of herself. If he wanted a marriage for Susie's benefit, he could have a marriage for Susie's benefit. She would be Susie's mother but she would not be his wife. Why should she allow him to humiliate her? Had he ever done anything else? She was sick and tired of being attacked with sins she had not committed. Sick and tired of the pain, sick and tired of the wayward emotions which kept on making her a target for more pain. This was never going to be a normal marriage. Cesare was not going to wake up some day and magically believe that she was an innocent victim. He had destroyed the evidence which she might have been able to use to establish her innocence. He had refused to listen to her. He had not once made the slightest effort to employ that brilliant mind on the startling idea that she might not be guilty as charged. Well, OK, fine...if that was how he was determined to play it, but Mina intended to embark on her own offensive.

She went downstairs an hour later, clad in denim Bermudas and a cerise tie blouse, both of which had retailed at chain-store prices. She had dumped every single scrap of the clothing he had bought her on the floor in his bedroom.

She ran Giulia to earth in a room off the vast kitchen and engaged her services as an interpreter so that she

could invite Cesare's housekeeper to show her round the
castello. Paolo, who turned out to be Maria's husband,
officially took charge of the tour. With Giulia trans-
lating as best she could, Mina struggling to pick up the
humble beginnings of a basic working vocabulary in
Italian and everyone cheerfully correcting her pronun-
ciation while answering her many questions, it was a
lengthy but surprisingly enjoyable exercise.

'So this is where you are.'

The animated conversation tailed away into silence.
Mina's amethyst eyes darkened and hardened on the sight
of Cesare poised in the doorway. 'I've been taking the
official tour,' she said.

'I planned to show you round.'

'As you see, it wasn't necessary.'

Her companions melted away like snow in summer,
subdued by the electric tension in the air. Cesare surveyed
Mina's defiantly set face, took in the outfit and elevated
an ebony brow. 'What are you playing at?'

'Well, I don't want to play at being your wife any
more,' Mina breathed flatly. 'I gave it a whirl and, let
me tell you, twenty-four hours was more than enough.'
A deep dark bitterness unlike anything she had ever
known lanced through her as she drew herself up to her
full diminutive height, quite untouched by the incredulous look stamped on Cesare's dark, vibrant features. 'The worm has turned, Cesare. I can't change the
way you feel about me but the good news is I don't care
any more! I don't give a damn what you think. Nor do
I have the slightest interest in what you say, what you
do or where you go!'

'I'm not going anywhere——'

'Oh, I expect you'll change your mind about that. If
you want what you call *personal* entertainment,' Mina
phrased in a tone of shaking rage, 'then you can go find
it elsewhere! As far as I'm concerned I'm not married
to you.'

Cesare surveyed her with blatant disbelief. 'Don't be ridiculous.'

'I'm not being ridiculous. Out of the utmost generosity of spirit, I decided to give you a second chance——'

'*You* decided to give *me* a second chance?' he practically whispered.

'And you blew it in one night. I was prepared to do the very best I could to make this a real marriage,' Mina told him rawly. 'I was not prepared to be greeted with a new series of threats and yet another one of your revenge fantasies——'

'My *what*?' Cesare roared at her.

'I hate your guts!' Mina splintered back at him with what was perfect truth at that precise moment, on the edge of leaping up and down with sheer uncontrollable rage. 'I wouldn't want your precious forgiveness if I was on the edge of the grave! And not if you were lying on that floor right now *dying* would you get my forgiveness for what you've done to me! I'm finished with you—absolutely, totally finished with you on a personal basis!'

There was an instant of sharp silence as she spat out those final syllables.

Eyes narrowed to a gleam of glancing gold beneath black lashes rested on her for a timeless moment and then, without the smallest warning, Cesare flung his arrogant dark head back and burst out laughing.

It was like throwing a match on a bale of hay. Mina went up in flames. Stalking across the room, she swung her hand back to slap him but he ducked with fluid speed and shot out two powerful hands to capture her wrists before she could pull back. Her teeth gritted, she attempted to kick him to force him to release her. He dropped his hands fast to her narrow ribcage and simply lifted her off the floor.

'*Put me down*!' she screeched at him as he held her at arm's length.

Rampant amusement sent a dazzling smile across his sensual mouth. 'I plead self-defence.'

Meeting that charismatic smile was like running into a brick wall at a hundred miles an hour. Rage turned to complete bewilderment. If she had been on her own feet, she would have swayed with dizziness, and while she was warring with that alarming reality Cesare brought her up to him and closed his arms round her.

'Put me down,' Mina mumbled in a different voice entirely.

'I have this appallingly sexist urge to kiss you,' he whispered in a thickened tone that sent tiny little shivers running down her spine.

'F-forget it.'

In blatant disagreement, Cesare rearranged her even more intimately against him, settling her arms down on to his shoulders and splaying his hands on the swell of her hips. He let his mouth nuzzle against the taut curve of her delicate jawbone and then probed the mutinously sealed line of her lips. She quivered, fighting what he could make her feel with every fibre of her being, terrified that she would respond.

Disconcertingly, hot, salty tears suddenly lashed her eyes and overflowed down her cheeks. She despised her own weakness, despised herself utterly for even being tempted. Wanting hurt, loving hurt, and she had allowed him to teach her those things.

Abruptly, Cesare lowered her back down to the floor. 'Mina?' He sounded shaken.

She dashed a furious hand across her wet cheeks and slung him a look of uninhibited loathing. 'I *hate* you!' she gasped in an ironic lie.

CHAPTER NINE

MINA gazed out over the valley. Near the *castello* the landscape was thickly wooded but further off she could see olive groves and orchards of orange and lemon trees. The wrought-iron bench she sat on stood in the dappled shade of a huge beech tree. The noisy exchanges of two goats tethered on opposing sides of the road far below briefly disrupted the silence. Mina sighed, charmed by the beauty of the peaceful scene but more troubled than ever by her own tangled thoughts.

She hadn't seen Cesare since yesterday. He had left her alone. She had asked for a tray in her room last night and had lain sleepless until long after midnight, ruefully reflecting on the truly mortifying reality that even fighting with him was preferable to being deprived of him altogether. She was deeply ashamed of that fact.

The soft crunch of footfalls turned her head. Cesare stilled several feet away, sunlight gleaming over his black hair and glancing off the hard angles of his classic profile. She tensed, disconcerted that he had tracked her down.

'This was my great-grandmother's favourite place,' he murmured in wry explanation. 'She died when I was thirteen. For a long time afterwards I would come here to feel close to her and I would still see her sitting there on that bench, dressed from head to toe in black. She was a wonderful old lady, very sharp, very shrewd.'

'You never talk about your family...' Mina stared at him.

'Bisnonna was the most important part of it,' Cesare told her, his mouth twisting as he looked out over the valley. 'When my grandparents died in a train crash, she raised my father. He married my mother when she was

146

twenty-one. I was born, then Sandro. My parents may have stayed together but it was a lousy marriage.'

Mina looked at him in astonishment. She remembered him saying that Susie deserved the very best that he could give her and that his parents had done that for him. It had not occurred to her that the best might have been less than perfect.

Cesare expelled his breath in a hiss and swung back to her, his strong features taut and clenched. 'Believe it or not, I don't want the same for us,' he told her with harsh emphasis. 'I don't want a charade for Susie's sake. You can't fool a child. She would sense the lack of warmth between us, feel the resentment, hear the silences...'

Mina bent her head. He had shaken her and she was suddenly gripped by raw tension as she wondered where the dialogue he had initiated was leading. It sounded very much to her as though he was about to admit that their marriage had been a bad idea, entered into in haste but not to be repented at leisure.

'You think we made a mistake,' she forced herself to say out loud.

'No...' The silence stretched as taut as a rubber band. 'I think *I* am the one who has made mistakes,' he contradicted grittily.

Her head flew up, startled amethyst eyes skimming to his fiercely set jawline. He still wasn't looking at her. But abruptly that changed. He spun fluidly round, dark-as-night eyes settling on her with perceptible force, a tiny pulse tugging at the edge of his unsmiling mouth, revealing the depth of his strain. 'It may be no consolation...but I'm not like this with anyone but you. I thought I'd put it all behind me but recognising you in that charity newsletter was like getting a shot of insanity in my veins. Four years ago you left me high and dry and feeling as foolish as an infatuated teenager. I was very bitter. Maybe this time I was trying to rewrite our history...'

'Yes,' Mina conceded, reeling from his blunt and raggedly voiced confession. Whatever her own private thoughts on the subject might have been, the depth of remembered bitterness in Cesare's delivery told her that he was recalling feelings that went far beyond the sting of a dented ego. He might not have loved her but he had been hurt and humiliated, she acknowledged, pained by that awareness, and if he would not believe her there was nothing she could do to take away those bitter memories. They would always stand between them.

'But that night at the benefit *everything* went haywire,' he intoned with a humourless laugh. 'Instantaneously I wanted you again. I looked at you and you looked back at me and I knew you felt the same way, even though I was an unwelcome and dangerous echo from the past.'

'I——' For a split-second she was on the brink of arguing the point out of pride and then she too remembered how she had felt. Her skin burned. That intense hunger had been mutual. Even when they were fighting like cat and dog that hunger remained.

'If you had admitted what you had done I would have behaved differently,' Cesare stressed, and as her lips parted he shifted an expressive brown hand in a silencing motion. 'I don't want to get into that again.'

'But——'

'Leave it in the past where it should have stayed,' he interposed in grim interruption. 'Who am I to talk about stainless-steel ideals? I've had money all my life. I've always been able to do whatever I wanted to do and I suppose I must take that for granted. I can understand that you were tempted——'

'But I——'

'*Dio* ... aren't there more important things?' Cesare shot at her with sudden raw frustration. 'Can't you see that this endless rehashing of the past is tearing us apart?'

Mina lost her angry colour, her stomach cramping up. 'I wasn't aware there was an us to be torn apart,' she said tightly.

The silence went on and on and on.

Cesare gazed back at her, very pale and taut, brooding dark eyes intently pinned to her. 'Finding out about Susie devastated me...'

'I should have told you,' Mina breathed in a guilty undertone. 'I should have told you when she was born.'

'I would have liked to have been there from the beginning,' he admitted very quietly. 'But now I've come to terms with the shock I'm simply grateful that she exists. I should have apologised before now for the accusations I made that afternoon. First impressions weren't on anyone's side and I wanted to hit back at you for keeping her a secret. You felt like the enemy that day.'

Mina nodded.

'First Clayton squaring up to me like a Viking version of a Rottweiler,' he recalled, 'then your sister behaving as if I were some maniac on the loose...and then out of nowhere...Susie! I was shattered but also blazingly angry with you. It was easier to ignore you and concentrate on Susie than risk dragging out those feelings before the wedding...'

She recognised what an effort it was for him to admit how angry and bitter he had felt—ironically much the same as she herself had felt until she'd blown a gasket yesterday and said a lot of things she didn't mean in a frantic last-ditch effort to save face. Yet what she had flung in anger had shaken Cesare enough to make him begin talking to her.

But then he was thinking about Susie, wasn't he? Clearly remembering his own less than idyllic childhood with unhappily married parents, he had been forced to see that he was doing everything possible to create the same situation.

'We didn't have any privacy at the manor.' But even as Mina said that she realised that both of them had avoided being alone together. Pride had made her equally guilty of a desire to avoid a direct confrontation and she had wanted Cesare to have time to simmer down. However, she'd really known deep down that, left to his own devices, he was more likely to boil than cool off.

'*Dio mio*, that is not a problem here at the *castello*, but then let's face it, we're not the average newly-weds.' Cesare vented a sardonic laugh that cut through her like a knife. 'We don't have to stay here if you don't want to. I have the villa we can use on the coast.'

Concessions, Mina thought, comprehension spiralling through her. Without ceremony, Cesare had laid aside his desire to punish her. It had finally dawned on him that he couldn't hurt her without hurting Susie as well. No wonder he looked so desperately on edge, and sounded so stilted: he was compromising those 'stainless-steel ideals', bending them for his daughter's benefit. Welcome to the marriage of convenience you thought you could settle for a few weeks ago, Mina reflected in an agony of pain.

'Mina...?'

'Whatever you like,' she said flatly, with the unspoken clarity of someone who didn't give a damn where they went.

'It's...nice.' Mina stared down fixedly at the twisted rope wedding-ring, her colour high. She imagined it turning into a real rope which she could pull tight round Cesare's throat. The image was so innately enervating that she snapped shut the jewel box again. Cartier's, she noted without surprise. Not a fake this time...but still an empty symbol, she told herself painfully.

'Try it on,' Cesare suggested.

'Later.' She thrust the box into her bag. She would put it in the drawer with his other gifts. She didn't want to wear them either. Cesare seemed to think that keeping her happy meant spending a fortune on jewellery. He had already given her a fabulous gold watch and an em-

erald and diamond bracelet...not to mention a hideous
stuffed fish in a glass case!

Freddy Fish, as she had christened him, had been an
experiment to see whether or not she was right to assume
that Cesare would buy absolutely anything she chose to
admire. So yesterday she had admired the fish in an an-
tique shop just to see how far he was prepared to go
with his current policy of extravagantly flashing his wallet
at every possible opportunity.

He had paled...but the grotesque fish had duly been
purchased at an outrageous price. And Cesare, dem-
onstrating a deviously disgusting desire to keep her sweet,
had even sunk low enough to say that Freddy was a fascinating rarity. To punish him, Mina had said how wonderful it would be if she could make a collection of such
things.

It was ten days since Cesare had tactlessly told her
that they were scarcely the average newly-weds. And
indeed they were not, Mina conceded miserably. Far
from lolling about in indolence and idyllic passion, they
had 'done' Sicily. From dawn to dusk, with Cesare in
relentlessly energetic mode, she had been culturally force-
fed with ruins, castles and cathedrals. They had spent
several nights at Cesare's luxurious villa on the coast.

At dusk, they generally went out for dinner, over which
they made very polite conversation or discussed Susie,
always a saviour when the conversation threatened to
flag or veer into controversial territory. And in the early
hours...they fell into their separate beds.

'I would like you to wear a wedding-ring,' Cesare delivered softly now.

It was a seriously challenging tone. In ten days
seriously challenging was the closest Cesare had allowed
himself to get to angry. He really was putting immense
effort into being civilised, charming and considerate. But
he was like a tiger in chains underneath the smooth front,
and with every passing day of such treatment Mina
became more depressed. She was convinced that Cesare

was secretly bored out of his mind with her. Yet nobody could deny that he was doing everything possible to make their marriage of convenience work for Susie's benefit.

'Mina,' he murmured.

'I don't want to wear a ring.'

For a split-second smouldering gold flared under the lush black lashes which she so envied and then he veiled his gaze. His sensual mouth compressed but he said nothing.

Mina watched him from behind her sunglasses. Breathtakingly good-looking and incredibly sexy and he didn't want her any more. Having taken revenge out of the equation, Cesare appeared to have found a complete cure for the hunger which he had assured her would never be satisfied. Presumably his desire for revenge had previously lent her a quality of challenging excitement which was now wholly absent. She now seemed to exude as much attraction for Cesare as Freddy Fish, she thought wretchedly.

He snapped his brown fingers for attention and settled the bill for their lunch. As he rose lithely upright, shrugging his broad shoulders back to straighten his jacket, Mina followed every fluid movement from behind the safe screen of her glasses. Her heartbeat was in earthquake mode, her breathing pattern shamefully fractured. In a devastatingly well-cut designer suit, his exquisitely tailored trousers defining every muscular line of his very long, lean legs, he held her entire attention.

'Something wrong?' he enquired lazily.

'Nothing!' Her voice emerged shrilly as she recalled him saying that on a physical response level he had been able to read her like a billboard four years ago. The idea that she might still be that easily read petrified her.

'I think it's time you met some of my friends,' he announced without warning. 'It would be a shame not to call in when we're practically on their doorstep.'

He made a call on his mobile phone before he swung into the Ferrari again. He dealt Mina a sizzling smile that made her skin prickle. 'I'm sure we'll have an entertaining afternoon with Franca and her brother. Franca's an actress. Roberto's a producer.'

The Ecchio villa looked remarkably like a building on an extravagant filmset. It was palatial, furnished with a preponderance of *faux* marble pillars and grand gilded furniture. They had only got as far as the giant foyer when a tall and stunningly beautiful brunette with a waist-length mane of curling dark hair appeared. She was wearing something very short and flimsy in leopard print. Her equally stunning figure gleamed with golden perfection through every strategic cut-out. Indeed the outfit was so arresting that Mina gaped.

She needn't have worried that her behaviour would be noticed. The brunette walked right past her as if she were invisible and fell on Cesare, kissing him passionately full on the mouth.

'Franca...' Cesare purred, making little attempt to detach himself from the indecently close press of that next-door-to-half-naked heavenly body.

Franca burst into a flood of exuberant Italian, slid an arm round him and proceeded to walk him away. Cesare replied at similar length and then glanced back with reluctance at Mina, prompting the actress finally to notice his companion.

'Tina needs to freshen up,' Franca said in perfect English, liquid dark eyes skimming over Mina's simple yellow sundress pityingly as she signalled to a maid-servant standing near by.

'It's Mina actually,' she responded with cheeks that burned hotter than hellfire.

But Franca had already turned back to Cesare to lead him away. 'The English dress so *badly*,' she was saying in a stage-whisper which could have been heard a mile away. 'Where on earth did you dig her up?'

Mina was shaking with shock and mortification by the time the maid had shown her into a cloakroom. She couldn't believe that Cesare had simply walked away with that woman without making the slightest attempt to introduce her as his wife.

She looked in the mirror at the linen-mix dress which was two seasons old. This morning it had been immaculate but now it was badly creased. She cringed. All of a sudden, not wearing the clothes Cesare had bought her seemed a stupid and childishly rebellious act. Maybe he had been too ashamed of her appearance to admit that she was his wife, she found herself thinking painfully.

She had to find her own way to the social gathering by following the sound of voices out to a fabulously landscaped outdoor pool. A passing waiter paused to offer her a drink from the laden tray he was carrying. Mina accepted a glass. Three young women were sunbathing topless by the pool. Mina had only ever sunbathed topless in her twin's presence . . . she could feel her skin turning brick-red again as she hurriedly glanced away from the surfeit of naked female flesh on display.

Cesare was seated at one of the tables beside Franca and several other men. Catching sight of Mina in the doorway, the brunette sprang up and advanced. 'Tina . . . let me show you the swimwear.' She planted a determined hand on Mina's spine and propelled her across the tiled floor into a luxurious changing-room.

'My name is Mina,' Mina said quietly.

'Whatever,' Franca dismissed imperiously, making no attempt to open any of the built-in storage units as she studied Mina with irritated dark eyes. 'You're his secretary or something, right?'

'Wrong.'

'You're a relative?' Franca pressed dubiously.

'No, we're——'

Franca gasped in horrified disbelief. 'He's not——?'

'I beg your pardon?' Mina was shattered by her crude assumption.

'I'll call a car for you. You should leave now,' Franca told her with a smile of suppressed rage. 'If I hadn't been away on location, you wouldn't have got a look-in! Cesare is *mine*.'

'I don't think so,' Mina retorted drily.

Franca spat something at her in voluble Italian, her magnificent breasts heaving against the flimsy beach cover-up. Then, disconcertingly, she laughed and dealt Mina a look of supreme scorn. 'Stay, then, and watch me in action.'

'I can hardly wait.'

'Cesare is a living legend between the sheets. I hear he's an animal in bed,' Franca purred with rich appreciation and enormous complacency. 'You couldn't begin to compete with me.'

With that parting shot, Franca departed. Exit stage left, Mina reflected, in no doubt that the flamboyant brunette was an actress after her theatrical display and decidedly relieved that Franca had apparently not had hands-on experience of Cesare's legendary attributes in the bedroom.

She drained her glass of champagne and dragged open one of the closets to rifle through the swimwear available. All of a sudden she was desperately keen to be rid of the yellow sundress. Ten minutes later, she emerged from the changing-room somewhat self-consciously sheathed in a brief black bikini with chain clasps on the hips and top.

'*Bella! Bella!*' a male voice exclaimed and a hand captured her wrist as she attempted to walk past his table and held her fast.

Bemused, she stared down at the man.

'I am your host, Roberto Ecchio... and, unlike my sister, I love British women.' He pressed a practised kiss to her inner wrist, shooting her a smouldering upward glance clearly intended to make her collapse gratefully at his feet.

Mina couldn't help it. She laughed.

He gave her a pained look, drawing her down on to the vacant chair beside him. 'You're in love with Cesare?'

'Mind your own business,' Mina told him, her attention roaming over to the far table where Cesare was in deep conversation with Franca, their dark heads intimately close. Her stomach cramped up, perspiration moistening her upper lip. It crossed her mind that, although she did not expect Cesare to stick to her like superglue in company, since they had entered the villa she could well have dropped dead without him noticing.

'Crazy about him,' Roberto Ecchio decided. 'What a waste of your emotion, *cara*. Cesare's a loner and not the faithful type. Here today, gone like greased lightning tomorrow. You'll never hold him. He's a professional heartbreaker.'

Mina tensed. 'How well do you know him?'

'We went to school together,' Roberto laughed, pushing a brimming glass towards her. 'A lot of women have cried on my shoulder about Cesare.'

'I'm not crying.'

'But you will.' Roberto cast a meaningful look in Cesare's direction. Franca was running a caressing finger playfully along his strong jawline and laughing at whatever he was saying. 'Franca's been after him for a long time and I'm afraid my sister doesn't listen to warnings. Don't worry about it. She'll get her fingers burnt too.'

'Very probably.' Mina wondered if Franca had deliberately set her brother on her to keep her away from Cesare. Not that Cesare was exactly fighting to escape the brunette's attentions.

'He's not the marrying kind.'

'He is,' Mina said gruffly. 'He's married to me.'

Roberto Ecchio looked at her fixedly.

'We got married ten days ago. Ask him if you don't believe me,' Mina continued defensively.

'Then what the hell is he playing at?' the other man demanded with a frown.

'Perhaps you should mention it to your sister.'

Roberto gave her a staggered glance and then bewil-
dered her by roaring with laughter. He snatched up her
hand again, surveyed her with eyes still alight with
dancing amusement and murmured, 'So very pleased to
make your acquaintance, Signora Falcone. But break
news like that to Franca when there's an audience around
to hear her hysterics? You have to be joking! As for
Cesare...he deserves to have the bars of his cage
rattled...'

With that incomprehensible assurance, Roberto Ecchio
carried her fingers up to his mouth and started kissing
them one by one.

Mina was so taken aback by his behaviour that she
froze and simultaneously collided with an electrifying
look of stunned censure from Cesare. Eyes across a
crowded room, she thought numbly—eyes that went for
the jugular would have been a more appropriate description. Abruptly freeing himself from Franca's
clinging hands, Cesare sprang upright. His vibrantly
handsome features a mask of dark fury, he thrust the
table out of his path. Mina was transfixed and she wasn't
the only one trapped in sudden paralysis. Everybody was
looking.

Roberto squinted sideways as he slowly raised his head,
even greater amusement marking his mobile face. 'So!
One violently jealous husband erupts out of nowhere!
Dio mio! Cesare Falcone, Mr Cool himself, so jealous
he makes a public scene,' he savoured smugly, lounging
back unconcerned in his seat. 'He won't hit me. I'm his
best friend.'

He was right. Cesare didn't hit him. He threw him in
the swimming-pool.

Somebody screamed. In a state of utter mute paralysis, Mina watched Roberto Ecchio hit the water with
an enormous splash and an expression of extreme shock.

'We're going home,' Cesare snarled, tugging Mina out
of her seat with one powerful hand.

'I've g-got to get my clothes!'

But Cesare wasn't listening, he wasn't hearing. His blazing golden eyes settled on her and he just grabbed her up into his arms like an unwieldy parcel and strode away from the poolside, leaving a deathly silence in their wake.

'*Cesare*!' Mina shrieked, and then the clasp on the front of her bikini came undone and she made a frantic dive to hold it in place over her heaving breasts.

The Ferrari went down the driveway like a rocket.

'Violently jealous'. In the thunderous silence, as Cesare took a corner on a wing and a prayer, tyres screaming in protest, Mina stole a wide-eyed look at the ferocious cast of his profile. 'Violently jealous'. She was dumb-struck by the concept. Yet she now saw that that same concept had been staring her in the face from the very moment of meeting Cesare again. Cesare went crazy if another man so much as looked at her. First Edwin Haland, then Steve . . . now his best friend who had been foolish enough to bait the tiger.

He had actually been jealous of Steve. No wonder he had been delighted to realise that her former boyfriend had never been her lover. His repeated references to Steve on their wedding night were now clarified. Cesare had been so inflamed with jealousy, he hadn't been able to think of any other solution beyond burying her alive in a remote Sicilian valley and preventing her from re-turning to England.

That was a demonstration of such innate insecurity that Mina was torn between helpless amusement and a kind of agonised tenderness on his behalf. She had been so blind, so pitifully hung up on the belief that she was not important to him. Only now did she see that her own insecurity had come between her and her wits. Cesare did not want to lose her . . . Cesare was *afraid* of losing her and she did not think that the volatile emotions he was struggling to control right now were anything to do with Susie.

So what on earth had he been playing at with Franca Ecchio? That didn't make sense. Why behave in a fashion guaranteed to cause trouble? For some extraordinary reason he had allowed Franca to come on to him like a man-eater while he ignored Mina.

A little smile softened the formerly strained line of Mina's mouth. Well, sixth sense told her that Cesare would not ignore her again in company, nor would he allow another woman to flirt like mad with him. He would be too busy watching a wife he clearly considered to be fatally attractive to other men and fighting off the competition. Perhaps there was something to be said for those irredeemably basic instincts of his. They cut right through that smooth, sophisticated and polished exterior and revealed the wonderfully human emotions that lurked secretively beneath.

He snatched her up out of the Ferrari outside their villa, roared through the front door, startling the maid fixing flowers in the hall, and carted her upstairs, kicking open the door to her bedroom.

He dropped her down on the bed and looked down at her with scorching golden eyes, hunger blatant in that electrifying stare. Intense awareness throbbed in the atmosphere between them, filling Mina with a sudden surge of heat, shooting every skin cell on to red alert.

Cesare drew in a deep, shuddering breath. 'Don't do that again,' he warned unevenly.

Considering his mood, it was an astonishingly mild reproof. He pushed an unsteady hand through his black hair. Momentarily he looked dazed, like someone waking up after a brainstorm. The phone buzzed. Lines of strain engraving his hard features, he backed away from her. His physical retreat was so unexpected, that Mina simply stared. He answered the phone. Dark colour demarcated his savage cheekbones. He uttered a forced laugh. '*Ciao*, Roberto.'

He dropped the receiver back onto the cradle.

Mina sat up, her skin drenched with hot pink.

'Tit for tat,' Cesare murmured darkly, his teeth gritted.

'P-pardon?'

'Ten days ago you told me to find another woman.' Mina turned pale. 'I did *what*?'

'I decided to test the water, see how you reacted...'

Belatedly she recalled all the foolish things she had thrown in that row, not one of which she had expected him to take seriously. Now it dawned on her that Cesare had believed her when she had urged him to entertain himself elsewhere. Horror gripped her, then incomprehension. Had Cesare been trying to make her jealous this afternoon?

'And you didn't like it—you didn't like it at all,' he drawled, but his teeth were still gritted. 'Until Roberto decided to throw a spanner in the works——'

'Why not? Franca is his sister!'

'He knows I wouldn't lay a finger on Franca. She's been throwing herself at me for years! It's a standing joke between us.'

'A standing joke?' Mina echoed, striving without success to see the gorgeous sexy brunette in that light.

'What else would it be? A teenager carrying on like a thirty-something vamp from an old movie!'

'A t-teenager?' Mina stammered incredulously. 'Franca's a *teenager*?'

'Famous and gloriously narcissistic, but then she is only nineteen.'

Nineteen... Mina was deprived of speech for the space of thirty seconds.

'But you knew I wouldn't realise what age she was! You took me there quite deliberately!' she accused. 'And as for you thinking that I would give you the freedom to stray, you've got another think coming, Cesare Falcone! Now I wish I'd pushed that conceited little madam into the pool!'

'She's a foot taller and at least two stone heavier. I would have had to wade in and rescue you, *bella mia*.' Cesare strolled lithely to the foot of the bed, glittering golden eyes skimming her outraged face. 'So if I don't have the freedom to stray, why the bloody hell did you tell me I did?' he suddenly raked at her fiercely.

'I didn't think you believed me . . . you *laughed*!'

'I didn't feel one bit like laughing when you started crying while I was trying to kiss you . . . and you know it!'

'I didn't know it.'

'I've been afraid to touch you ever since! You made it painfully clear that you didn't want me,' he bit out unevenly.

Her eyes stung, making her drop her head. Both of them had been too busy hiding behind their pride, refusing to give an inch. Yet Cesare had given so much in so many other ways, she acknowledged for the first time. It wasn't his fault that she had felt so rejected she had frozen him out on every possible occasion. Sometimes, she registered, loving meant putting your pride on the line.

'For ten bloody frustrating days you have been totally unresponsive to my every attempt to make you happy,' he condemned in a driven undertone.

It was true. Like a sulky child, she had stonewalled him with petty gestures of defiance, hugging her pain to herself, refusing to show it.

'I can't do anything right with you,' he grated.

The tears stung even harder behind her lowered eyelids. 'I always want you,' she whispered. 'Seems to me I never learned how to stop that——'

The silence hung like a deadened weight above her head. She bit her lip and tasted blood, feeling exposed.

'Say that again,' Cesare invited unsteadily.

She sniffed. 'You heard me.'

He hunkered down to her level and reached out for her tightly clasped hands. She kept her eyes closed, willing back the moisture, strengthened by the warm feel of his hands enclosing hers. It felt so good even though his hands weren't quite steady. She swallowed hard. She had been alone for a long time. She had put up so many barriers over the last four years. Once she had been open, outspoken, had known no better than to wear her heart on her sleeve. Only now did she admit that she had not hidden behind pride with Cesare. She had hidden behind the terrible fear of being hurt again. And when you were scared you didn't give generously.

She would never have made the slip of telling him that she loved him again had she not been mindless with passion in his arms. But his outright rejection of that love had cut deep. 'You don't believe anything I say,' she reminded him tightly.

'I'm learning,' Cesare breathed very quietly, holding her hands tightly in his as if he was scared that she was about to make a break for freedom.

'Is Roberto ever going to forgive you?'

'I owe him an Armani suit. He's a good sport.'

'He was just...just joking around.'

'*Sì*...I know, but coming after these last days...the strain...' Cesare sighed heavily '...I blew a fuse.'

She looked down at his lean, beautifully shaped brown hands and an intense tide of love surged up inside her. It really didn't matter if he didn't love her. It really didn't matter if her only hold on him was sex and the daughter they shared. There were a lot of shades between white and black and she could settle for mid-grey and make the best of it, because the most terrifying truth of all had to be faced. Without him there was nothing.

'Let me tell you about Steve,' she suggested, badly needing to lay that ghost for good and all.

'No, I don't want to talk about the past,' Cesare asserted at speed.

'But——'

He laid a fingertip against her lower lip. 'No,' he said again, with an edge of harshness.

Unwarily she opened her eyes, and sank dizzily into burnished gold. The conversation went right back out of her head.

'Stay the night with me,' he whispered, raising a hand and brushing his knuckles gently across one damp cheekbone.

'It's only four in the afternoon ...'

'I'm booking you in advance.'

'I kind of like you on your knees,' Mina dared.

'It's the only time we're eye to eye and still vertical,' Cesare pointed out sardonically.

'We have to ring Susie ...'

'We'll be with her tomorrow,' he reminded her, leaning forward, gathering her up and easing her closer.

Her bones turned liquid. He brushed his mouth very softly over her parted lips and she stopped breathing. Her heartbeat hammered crazily. Her hands slid up to caress his hard cheekbones. As he pressed her back, the newspaper lying on the bed behind her crackled noisily. Lifting his head, Cesare wrenched it out from beneath her to toss it aside and then tensed, every muscle of his powerful physique pulling ferociously taut.

'What?'

Even as she spoke, Cesare was already coiling back from her. The newspaper still gripped in his hand, he sprang upright. *'Madre de Dio ...'* he breathed.

Mina frowned. 'What's wrong?'

His concentration was entirely fixed on the English newspaper she had been reading over breakfast earlier in the day. A tiny muscle jerking at the corner of his compressed mouth, he lifted his head again, all his natural colour drained from his dark skin. 'Didn't you see this?' he demanded.

'See what?'

He flipped the paper to exhibit a photo beside an article. 'That's Severn.'

'Who?' she whispered.

'The broker you used four years ago has been arrested for serious fraud!' Cesare spelt out rawly.

'Severn is the broker whom ...' Mina put together uncertainly.

A spasm of incredulous frustration crossed Cesare's taut, set features. 'What's the matter with you? Don't you realise what this means? Severn is under investigation! The police will have seized all his papers and they will be going through them, seeking out evidence with which to prosecute him and anyone else involved in his illicit dealing!'

'But... but I didn't...' Mina muttered shakily.

'Mina.' Cesare gripped her hand fiercely. 'You have to face reality sometime. I suggest you face it now... although for the first time in my life I am not sure that honesty is always the best policy,' he completed unevenly.

CHAPTER TEN

'I HOPE we do not live to regret this,' Cesare asserted grimly as the jet landed with a nasty judder. 'I don't think it was a good idea for you to return to London right at this moment.'

Mina said nothing. She hadn't got a wink of sleep last night. Cesare had reduced her to a state of mute terror. Being convinced of one's innocence was not a bar to fear, not when you had Cesare around, fully convinced of one's guilt. Cesare had brooded aloud on every possible worst-case scenario and then decided that she should never, ever set foot on British soil again!

It was small consolation to discover that she had a husband prepared to spend the rest of his days helping her to evade the long arm of the law. If he told her any more about the Statute of Limitations and the unlikelihood of extradition she would climb the walls, she reflected miserably.

Cesare was ready to do anything to keep her out of prison. He had toyed with the idea of her making a full confession and then decided that there was absolutely no way she would receive a fair trial as his wife. What jury could possibly have sympathy for a rich bitch? he had asked her, and he had gone on to cite instances where he believed that other wealthy women had been more heavily punished than would have been the case had they simply been more ordinary mortals.

He saw discovery and subsequent prosecution as inevitable, although it might take many months for evidence incriminating her to come to the fore in the police investigation, he had told her. On the other hand, since black pessimism seemed to be the order of the day, Mina knew that if the police were waiting for them on the tarmac as the jet landed he would probably not be too surprised, which was one of the main reasons why he had wanted to return alone to collect Susie.   –

Mina was in turmoil. Just when everything had been coming together for them, this had blown up in their faces: her supposed fraud. She had gone beyond bitterness but it did seem unnecessarily cruel that what had wrecked her life four years previously should now return to haunt her with even worse fears. If Cesare could not credit for one second that she was innocent, how the heck could she expect the police to believe her?

And how on earth could she feel confident when she sensed that Cesare was frantic on her behalf? Cesare... frantic and worried sick. Not something she had ever thought to witness. That scared her even more, because it underlined the seriousness of her situation. What was the point of repeatedly reiterating her innocence to him? And what were the chances that the real culprit would somehow be dug out of the woodwork and forced to answer for his crime? For his *two* crimes, Mina adjusted tautly. After all, a serious offence had been committed against her. She had been deliberately set up and falsely accused. But why? Why had someone taken the trouble to do that? The true offender could not have known that his broker would be arrested four years down the line and thus expose him to the possibility of prosecution.

Her head was aching so badly by the time they reached the limousine that, once inside, she rested her head back and closed her eyes, hoping to ease the throb of unbearable tension behind her temples.

Cesare reached out and closed his hand around hers. 'I can't let you go through this,' he said abruptly, harshly.

'What are you——?'

'We can't live with this threat hanging over us,' he contended with hard emphasis. 'I find it easier to meet trouble head-on rather than wait for it to find me. I will tell the police that I was the prime mover in the fraud and that you acted on my instructions.'

Her lashes swept up in shock. 'No... nobody's going to believe that!'

'Why not? Being wealthy does not mean that one cannot also be greedy,' Cesare retorted. 'An employee in love with her boss... it is credible that you could have been persuaded to break the law on my behalf. In fact if you acted dumb you could probably persuade the police that you didn't even know that what you did was illegal and you can't be forced to testify against me——'

Mina had jerked upright again. 'But you can't take the blame for it!'

Cesare studied her intensely, his jawline clenching hard. 'If it comes to prison, I could handle it. I don't think you could.'

Her throat closed over. She met those brilliant dark eyes of his in a full-tilt collision. Cesare was not the sacrificial type, no martyr to anyone else's cause, and there was a terrible irony in the fact that he would not have considered committing such an offence—no, not even if the reward had been millions. She was devastated by the lengths he was prepared to go to in order to protect her. It was not as though he believed her innocent, not as though he believed she had been led astray by someone else.

'Susie could get by without me for a while... but not without you,' he pointed out wryly. 'Meanwhile, just to hedge our bets, you get pregnant——'

'Pregnant?' Mina echoed, sinking into an even deeper daze of incredulity.

'If I confess and you are pregnant it makes your prosecution even less likely,' he said drily.

Her throat thickened with tears. 'You can't do it,' she said flatly. 'I won't let you do it. This is my problem, not yours!'

'You're my wife——'

'What the hell does that have to do with it?' Mina
slung at him in unhidden distress, and then she realised—
or thought she realised—and the suspicion that occurred
to her shook her inside out. Did he love her? Or did he
simply see protecting her and Susie as his duty?

'Everything.' His lean fingers tightened fiercely on hers
as he tugged her inexorably across the distance separ-
ating them.

Her tension suddenly gave way and with a muffled
little moan, she threw herself into the heat and solidity
of him, her hands frantic to touch, to hold and in some
way repel the fear threatening to consume her. All she
could see was their lives being ripped apart. 'You can't,'
she told him and she meant it, knew that no matter what
happened there was no way she was going to hide behind
him.

'*Bella... bella mia*, have a little sense.' With his thumb
he rubbed at the bloodless line of her compressed mouth
in reproof.

Her lips parted tremulously, the drugging heat of
awareness leaping through her like sudden fire, inflamed
by more than an edge of sheer desperation.

'We should have made better use of last night,' Cesare
muttered raggedly. 'I want you so much, I ache...'

Without warning, he pulled back from her and communicated with the chauffeur.

'What are you doing?'

'It'll take over an hour in this traffic to reach the town
house...'

Minutes later he was tugging her out of the limousine
in front of a well-known hotel. Ten minutes after that
they were standing in a luxurious bedroom.

'This is crazy,' Mina protested weakly.

'Everything I do with you is crazy,' he muttered
thickly, hauling her into his arms.

He took her mouth with a wild, surging hunger. She
went under like a novice swimmer, overwhelmed by the
swirling currents of unashamed passion and sucked down

mindlessly into the depths. But all the time her hands were busy. She wrenched off his jacket, embarked on his shirt buttons.

With a groan of frustration, Cesare drew back and dispensed with his own clothing. 'Someday we are going to do this with control and finesse!' he swore.

'But not today.'

'No, not today,' he agreed, pulling her back to him, impatient fingers locating the zip on her elegant summer dress.

He skimmed the dress down her arms and it pooled at her feet. He took in the satin and lace brevity of her lingerie, dark eyes blazing molten gold. '*Dio*...I have incredibly good taste.'

Mina was headily flushed. '*You* went shopping?'

'It kept me going before the wedding...when I had nothing else.'

He found her reddened mouth hungrily again and backed her down on the bed. A fire raging out of control could not have been more dangerous than the sudden scorchingly intimate connection they made. Theirs was an electrifying passion made all the wilder as the unleashed emotions ruling them both took over.

She lost herself in him. Her heart hammering, her slender body writhed beneath his, desperate for the completion that only he could give. She clutched at his hair, scored the satin-smooth skin of his back and then arched and sobbed as he sank into her in one powerful thrust.

'Nobody is going to take you away from me,' he said savagely, scanning her with glittering golden assurance. 'Nobody!'

And after that there was nothing but the hot, surging pleasure which drove her relentlessly up to the heights and then dropped her again into the valley of sobbing satisfaction.

'We are crazy to be doing this in the midst of a crisis,' Cesare conceded lazily a long time later as she lay wrapped in his arms, blissfully satiated, never, ever wanting to move again. 'But even if it can only be for a few hours, I want nothing else to intrude between us.'

Mina climbed back into the limousine feeling like a woman reborn. She felt strong, she felt good, she felt wonderfully liberated from her darkest fears. It was an extraordinary feeling. But she was less afraid of the police than she was of losing Cesare. Of course she would not allow him to step in and try to take the heat for her. He could make as many plans as he liked towards such an end but Mina knew that she would foil him if he made any such attempt.

But he had to care about her, he really had to care to be this concerned, this determined, this protective. He didn't need to say the words. At that moment she didn't mind if he never said the words. All the emotion he struggled to conceal had been communicated by his lovemaking. That hadn't just been sex. There had been an intense closeness between them that went far beyond anything they had ever shared. The barriers had come down. Cesare was hers in exactly the way she had always wanted him to be. Hook, line and sinker hers...and with that behind her she could face anything, she told herself.

'I have a few calls to make,' he imparted before they got out of the car outside the town house. 'Then we'll go down and pick up Susie. You will fly straight back to Sicily and tomorrow morning I will approach the police——'

'*No!*' Mina objected, dragged from her blissful inner world with a vengeance.

'It is imperative that I go to them before they come to you. They may well have been covertly investigating Severn for months,' Cesare pointed out grimly, and gripped her hand.

'I am not going back to Sicily,' Mina asserted tautly, and yanked her fingers free. 'I will go to the police. I don't want you involved——'

Her voice was cut off as the chauffeur opened the door. Mina scrambled out and walked into the town house, smiling tautly at the manservant who greeted her. As she entered the hall, Cesare powering up close behind with his long, impatient stride, an older woman appeared. She was very elegantly dressed and her ash-blonde hair was beautifully styled.

'Where have you been?' she demanded of Cesare, her face distraught. 'You left the airport five hours ago and I've been trying to reach you ever since!'

'What's wrong?' Cesare questioned tautly.

The older woman bit back a sob and breathed in convulsively. 'Your brother's been arrested——'

'*Di che cosa parli*?' Cesare raked.

'English, Cesare,' the woman stressed shakily.

'Sì Mamma...English,' Cesare rasped, and pushed open the door to a sunlit drawing-room. 'So what has Sandro done? Another car smash? I hope there is nobody injured this time——'

'He's in much deeper water than that!'

'Mina...allow me to introduce you to my mother, Louise Falcone,' Cesare breathed heavily.

'Didn't you hear what I said?' his mother shot at him hysterically, in no fit state to acknowledge her new daughter-in-law.

Cesare closed the door. Mina hovered uncomfortably, wondering if she should leave mother and son in private, wondering why Cesare had never mentioned the fact that his mother was English and not Italian.

'Sandro's been arrested for fraud!' the older woman told them, stricken.

'*Fraud*?' Cesare exclaimed incredulously.

'He had a partner. He was arrested last night. Sandro was picked up at the airport early this morning.'

Mina was as still as a statue but her brain was ticking over at supersonic speed.

Cesare cleared his throat. 'Are you telling me that Sandro was involved with Felix Severn?'

'Heavily involved.' Louise Falcone sank down heavily on to a chair, suddenly looking exhausted. 'He came to me before he went to the airport. He was so terrified, he told me everything.'

'And would everything include...insider dealing?' Cesare prompted unsteadily. Mina's gaze flew to his carved profile but there was nothing to be read there.

'That's the least of it,' his mother moaned. 'He's also been embroiled in several crooked deals in the insurance field. Severn was the front man. Sandro stayed in the background, putting up the finance, drumming up contacts...but you don't need to worry——'

'*I* don't need to worry?' Cesare repeated in a savage undertone. 'Mamma, if only you knew!'

'Sandro hasn't implicated Falcone Industries in any way!' his mother stressed, keen to make that point.

'I removed him from the board three years ago...how could he?'

'You humiliated him,' Louise condemned, her face twisting resentfully.

'But he was already up to his throat in crooked deals at that point, was he not?' Cesare pressed.

'Yes but how did you know that? Oh, what does it matter?' the older woman mumbled wearily. 'At least you're here now. Your lawyer is at the police station with him. I fixed that. You can arrange bail——'

'The legal system is different here. In any case, if the police picked him up at the airport, he'll be kept in custody. Sandro will run if he gets the chance...'

'Cesare...what's the matter with you?' Louise Falcone lifted her head and stared accusingly at her elder son. 'This is your brother we're talking about. He needs your help and support.'

Mina's knees were wobbling. Reeling with shock, she slumped down on to a chair and studied the carpet. It could only have been Sandro who set her up four years ago. But why? Why had Sandro done that to her? To cover his own tracks? Had he been afraid that Cesare either was or would become suspicious of his activities?

Or had there been a more personal element in his choice of her as the victim? Sandro had certainly disliked and resented her for repeatedly brushing off his approaches. That resentment could well have flamed into outrage that morning in the penthouse apartment when he realised that she had spent the night with his brother. Mina covered her chilled face with trembling hands.

'Sandro has never broken the law before,' his mother proclaimed in his defence.

'But he's lied all his life,' Cesare murmured so faintly that Mina had to strain to hear him.

'He needs our help and understanding!' Louise gasped. 'You can't turn your back on him. He's your brother!'

'*Mea culpa*——'

'Oh, don't start talking in Italian again!' his mother said shrilly.

'It was Latin——'

'Whatever. You're so *foreign*, Cesare. You're like your father. I've never been able to understand you and now my poor, sweet Sandro——' Louise broke down into hysterical sobbing.

With difficulty Mina dragged herself forcibly from shock and stood up. 'Cesare, I think you should go to the police station.'

His eyes were winter-dark and bleak, his superb bone-structure painfully prominent beneath his skin. 'What do I say now to you?' he muttered thickly.

Mina moved closer, understanding that, like her, Cesare was fathoms-deep in shock and aeons from any ability to feel concern for Sandro's predicament but he also had to appreciate that his mother had no idea why he should feel like that.

'The evidence in the file he gave me seemed fool-proof,' he murmured unevenly, thrusting splayed fingers through his thick black hair. 'Your signature, your voice on a taped phone call, the bank statements. He went to a lot of trouble over that file. Forgery... the tape must have been doctored, the statements you explained——'

'Not now.' Mina had to pitch her voice to be heard above his mother's sobs. 'Save it for later. It's not important.'

'Not important?' Cesare repeated dazedly.

'Look, do what you have to do first... for your mother's sake,' Mina urged.

'Susie's waiting for us,' he mumbled, visibly finding it an effort to concentrate.

'I'll pick her up and bring her back here... after I've sat with your mother for a bit,' Mina sighed. 'I can't leave her like this.'

'But——'

Mina gave him a helpful little push in the direction of the door. 'Find out what's happening at the police station.'

Her heart went out to him. She had never seen him in such a state of bewilderment. He simply wasn't func-tioning. Like a record stuck in a groove, he could focus only on the issue that was central to his marriage. 'You didn't do anything!' he said with sudden harshness. 'And all this time I've been——'

'Right now you are going to the police station to en-quire after your brother,' Mina informed him, ushering him out into the hall, dimly wondering if he was in any fit state to enquire after anyone. Shock had wiped him out. 'For your mother's sake,' she said again.

His expressive mouth curved bitterly. '*Sì...*'

'So unemotional, so judgemental... how did I give birth to a son like that?' Louise Falcone appealed tear-fully to Mina. 'Sandro's the complete opposite.'

While marvelling that any mother could make such a blatant favourite of Sandro with Cesare around, Mina took charge. She had coffee brought in and she located a box of tissues for her mother-in-law, who had by then surrendered completely to the need to establish what a wonderful son Sandro had always been.

Mina sat with a wooden smile through it all, her sympathies firmly with Cesare for having a mother so absorbed in one son that she had no time for the other. The afternoon crept away until Louise complained of a headache and decided to go and lie down. Mina mentioned that her daughter was waiting for her.

'I always wanted a little girl. Cesare is such a disappointment,' his mother lamented helplessly.

'Not to me,' Mina said brittly, having held her tongue as long as she could bear, but it washed off her mother-in-law completely.

The drive down to Thwaite Manor was the first chance Mina had to assimilate the devastating change that had taken place in her marriage. She smiled. It was as if an enormous weight had fallen off her shoulders. Cesare knew the truth now. He finally knew the truth. Sandro had clearly presented him with a very impressive body of evidence and her own apparent disappearance had played into Sandro's hands.

She didn't blame him for believing Sandro. She had only had one night with him. Family was family and she suspected that all his life Cesare had been made to feel protective towards his infinitely weaker brother. What reason would he have had to distrust Sandro?

When she arrived at the manor Susie surged into her arms and hugged her tightly. 'Where's my daddy?' she demanded.

'You'll see him soon,' Mina promised. 'We're going straight back to London.'

'Wonderful,' Winona remarked, avidly reading the details of Sandro's arrest in the evening paper. 'I hope they throw the book at the creep after what he did to you! How's Cesare taking it?'

'He's pretty shocked.'

'I bet he is.' Winona sighed, looking wry. 'But blood is thicker than water. I would believe you quicker than I would believe anyone else. But right now Cesare must feel like the ground has vanished beneath his feet.'

When Mina and Susie reached the town house, it was late. Susie was half asleep and Mina put her straight to bed. When she came downstairs again, Louise was talking angrily on the phone. Her face frozen with fury, she cut off the call, caught sight of Mina standing in the doorway and snapped, 'I'm not staying here. I'll stay at Sandro's apartment!'

Mina frowned. 'But why?'

'Cesare's not doing a damned thing to help his brother!' Louise hissed resentfully, and stalked off. Mina attempted to reason with the older woman but she wouldn't listen.

It was after eleven when she finally heard the front door opening. She leapt up as Cesare appeared in the doorway. He looked exhausted.

'Your mother's gone,' Mina told him.

Cesare shrugged. 'Probably for the best. I'm not going to work any miracle on Sandro's behalf. He's facing very serious charges. It's very unlikely that he'll get off without a prison sentence.'

'Did you see him?'

'No. However,' he sighed, 'he admitted what he had done four years ago to my lawyer and asked him to pass it on to me.' Mina's surprise was unhidden and Cesare released a bitter laugh. 'Why should he think of us in the midst of all his trouble?' he asked for her. 'I'll tell you why. The news that we're married has panicked my brother into the belief that I *already* knew that he had falsified the evidence against you. He chose to admit the deception in the hope of retaining my sympathy and support.' He framed the final three words with deadly cold finality.

'Why did he do it?' That was all Mina wanted to know.

'Apparently you heard him talking on the phone in the penthouse apartment the morning after we spent the night together.'

Mina didn't understand. 'Yes...but——'

'Evidently Sandro was involved in a highly confidential and dangerous call to Severn when you interrupted him. He was afraid that you had heard too much and would tell me when I returned from Hong Kong. The die was cast in that moment. He had to find some way to ensure that I got rid of you...'

Mina uttered a shaky little laugh and sank down on a seat. It was so simple that she would never have guessed. Sandro *had* been on the phone when she'd come out of the bedroom but she hadn't picked up a single word of what he had been saying. Her mind had been on other things. She had been deeply embarrassed by the discovery that the voice she had assumed to be Cesare's was in fact his brother's. Now she could recall how shocked Sandro had been when he had first turned to look at her that day, but she had naïvely misread what lay behind that shock.

'In the space of forty-eight hours he paid someone to forge your signature and someone else to doctor that tape. He had Severn's voice on tape and he was able to acquire yours. The two were spliced. If the fraud had been exposed, Sandro would have been in the clear. He was too greedy to put more than fifty thousand into your bank account...and no, I don't know whether he actually got that money back,' Cesare told her heavily. 'He didn't cover that aspect with my lawyer. When he had compiled the file, he flew out to Hong Kong to present me with it in person.'

'I had no idea...'

'I was already wondering what was wrong. Sandro had called me to inform me that you had gone on leave without clearing it with anyone. Since you didn't have a phone at home, I had no immediate way of contacting you. I was worried,' Cesare revealed tautly. 'I thought you might be upset and I blamed myself for not having talked to you that morning before I left.'

'But I was in the office... I didn't take any leave!' Mina protested.

'I know that now but I didn't at the time.'

'So you didn't phone,' Mina whispered in belated understanding and she could still remember how agonising that wait for a call had been. Cesare's silence had tormented her and made her suspect that he regretted their brief intimacy, just as Sandro had forecast.

'Sandro took one hell of a risk. If you had contacted me direct——'

'But I wouldn't have done that.' Mina repeated what his brother had said to her that morning.

Cesare paled and swung away. 'In Hong Kong he told me that he had heard you on the phone some days earlier and suspected that you might be passing on confidential information. He presented the file of evidence as the results of his investigation. He never once intimated that he had any idea that you and I were already lovers. I was shattered by that file,' he confided roughly.

The silence weighed heavily between them.

'I had you on a pedestal. I thought you were perfect. You were clever and gutsy and sexy, everything I ever wanted in a woman and I was crazy about you.' Cesare swung back round to face her, strained dark eyes bleak in his set features. 'But I'd always been pretty much of a cynic about love and marriage. My mother married my father for his money. He worked himself into an early grave maintaining her in the style to which she was determined to become accustomed and from time to time she had other men as well. When Sandro gave me that file, I thought that underneath I had to be as stupid and blind in love as my father once was!'

Her eyes prickled. 'Cesare, I don't——'

'So the first thing I did to prove I was no wimp was sack you out of hand,' Cesare continued with bitter derision. 'I wanted to cancel the rest of my trip and fly back but I wouldn't let myself do that. I was scared I needed to see you for the wrong reasons, so I made myself wait, and then when I did try to see you you had vanished!'

'Which must have made me look even guiltier,' Mina conceded before telling him that she had been on the brink of moving into a flat at the time and had not had the money to stay on in London.

'I felt guilty for hating Sandro for producing that file, especially when I felt I ought to be congratulating him for doing something constructive for once! But then I've always felt guilty about Sandro,' Cesare admitted with a grim twist of his expressive mouth. 'Only a year apart, we should be almost as close as twins, but we don't have a thing in common and never have had.'

'That happens in lots of families,' Mina murmured ruefully.

'He was a sickly baby and my mother's pet. I was very protective of him when we were children. But when he grew up no matter what he did he made a mess of it and that made me feel even worse because I knew he was always comparing himself to me. He hates me, he always has. He tries to hide it but he can't,' Cesare volunteered wryly. 'And if I'm honest, I'm not much keener on him and he was a constant embarrassment in Falcone Industries.'

'I gather he isn't a director any more.'

'I threw him out six months after I sacked you. Two of the secretaries came to me and lodged a complaint of sexual harassment against him.' Cesare's eyes hardened at the recollection. 'He had been behaving in the most disgusting manner towards them. His language and his conduct was utterly indefensible. He openly admitted it to me and actually laughed about it. He flatly refused to apologise and reform his behaviour. I set him up in his own company to get rid of him.'

'Must have been a relief all round.' Mina decided that now was not the time to horrify Cesare with the news that she too had once been the cringing target of Sandro's foul-mouthed and unwelcome attentions.

'It was. The whole atmosphere on the top floor changed. But, let's face it, people in glass houses should not throw stones,' he muttered tautly, and looked at her, a dark tide of colour drenching his hard cheekbones. 'When I finally found you again I too behaved in an indefensible manner. I was so scared that you would somehow end up making a fool of *me* again, I went off the rails and——'

'I know that,' Mina interrupted. 'But nothing you did puts you on a par with your creepy brother.'

'But I behaved like a maniac let loose! I wanted you back. I didn't much care how I did it either,' he conceded with self-loathing.

The silence stretched tautly.

Cesare searched her with dulled golden eyes. 'How do I say sorry for messing up your whole life?'

'Sandro messed it up. I can understand that you were presented with some very powerful evidence against me,' Mina told him soothingly.

'Absolutely everything I have ever done with you has gone wrong. What the hell did you feel like when I suddenly sacked you after that night we shared?' he demanded unsteadily.

'Pretty much the way you felt when Sandro gave you that file. Shattered.'

'And when you found out you were pregnant?' he prompted tautly.

'Multiply shattered by ten.'

'How the heck can you joke about it?'

'Because it's a long time ago and I know you tried to find me, even though you thought I had betrayed you.'

'Since I now know you were not partying,' he phrased, his mouth compressed with strain, 'and I wouldn't ask while we were in Sicily because I was scared you would tell me what I would have thought were more lies, it's time you told me how you did manage.'

She did, quietly and unemotionally. Cesare still looked devastated by guilt and she wished he hadn't bothered raising that particular subject. He was carrying enough of a burden in that field.

When she'd finished he cleared his throat awkwardly. 'That scar...' he began. 'Was that from having Susie?'

'Yes.'

'Tell me about it.'

'Why?'

'I ought to have been there. You might have died,' he muttered unevenly.

'Rubbish. It's a very common procedure,' Mina informed him bracingly. 'I didn't even have to be knocked out.'

'What do you mean?'

'I was conscious when she was born. They just put up a sheet...'

Cesare looked at her in unconcealed horror. '*Conscious*?' he echoed, turning an alarmingly pasty colour, moistening his lips and swaying. '*Dio*...that's medieval...'

Then, under her astonished scrutiny, Cesare collapsed down in a large heap on the Persian rug. He had passed out.

Mina loosened his tie and unbuttoned his jacket, torn between laughter and tears. Something told her that he would not have been a great deal of use at Susie's delivery. He swam back to the land of the living, blinking rapidly, sheepish as hell.

'I didn't feel a single twinge,' Mina assured him.

He was anything but convinced. 'To do *that* to you when you were still awake,' he mumbled with a sick shudder.

'I think you're dead on your feet. You should be in bed.'

He sat up. 'I'm fine.'

'You don't look it.' Mina took charge, feeling immensely superior, which was a bit mean but excusable. The sight of Cesare turning white to the gills and folding up would be an image she would never forget.

'I told you, I'm fine, and we still have a lot to talk about,' he argued as she pushed him towards the stairs.

'Tomorrow.'

'I can't wait that long. Where did you put Susie?'

He tiptoed into the dark bedroom and gazed down at his daughter. 'Did she miss me?'

'Loads,' Mina whispered from the doorway

'She ties my heart up in knots,' he muttered jerkily.

'She won't if you wake her up. She's very crabby when she's disturbed.'

He pulled the door shut again with exaggerated care and then hovered as though he was lost in his own house. 'I've made a mess of our marriage...'

'You tried hard to.' Mina didn't prevaricate. 'You hit your lowest point with Freddy Fish——'

'Freddy who?'

'I set you up with that fish to see how far you were prepared to go on your being nice campaign!'

A rawly appreciative smile momentarily wiped the tension from his vibrantly handsome features. 'You mean...?'

'I think the day Freddy was caught he should have been eaten or thrown back in the water. How dare you believe I had such bad taste? Your other low point was Franca the man-eating teenybopper...'

Cesare visibly winced. 'I was getting desperate...'

'But I never knew *how* desperate until you opened that newspaper and saw that Felix Severn had been arrested. *That*, in my opinion, was when you really went off the rails.' Mina strolled into the bedroom she had selected for herself, a grin etched on her beautiful face. 'Well, are you coming in or aren't you?' she asked mockingly when he paused on the threshold, being Cesare no doubt reading significance into her choice of a separate bedroom.

He came in, his eyes fiercely pinned to hers, a faint frown-line etched between his brows as he waited tensely to see what she was about to say next.

'Yes, you were like a man possessed with a mission last night,' Mina continued cheerfully. 'I got a vision of being holed up behind barricades in the *castello* ... the forces of law and order trying to starve us out!'

'Maybe I was a little over the top but naturally I was concerned,' he protested.

'Concerned?' Mina repeated shakily, struggling to hold back her amusement at this staggering piece of macho understatement. 'Cesare, by the time we landed in London you were a man on the very edge of lawlessness, ready to perjure yourself for my benefit!'

'*Dio mio* ... I didn't want you to go to prison!'

'But your determination to keep me out of the hands of the Fraud Squad really reached its crowning climax when you decided that you would be the sacrifice instead,' Mina completed, and had to swallow back a sudden thickness in her throat, her momentary amusement banished. 'Cesare, that was *so* sweet——'

'*Sweet*?' Dark colour delineated his blunt cheekbones, his lustrous dark eyes flaring gold at a label he found grossly inappropriate.

'I was touched to the heart. I also realised——'

'That only a man in love would make such an idiot of himself!' Cesare slotted in harshly, defensively. 'Well, why shouldn't you laugh?'

'I'm not laughing,' Mina whispered, distressed that he had taken her words the wrong way. She had hurt his feelings, pierced his pride and the wound was that much more tender for a male who found it hard to express those same feelings.

'I've always loved you,' he muttered almost defiantly. 'And thinking you were dishonest, grasping and that my only hold on you was sexual didn't make any difference. I was willing to settle for what I could get...'

Her nose tickled with the onset of tears. She remembered him voicing that same statement on their wedding night, and only now appreciated the significance of that admission.

'But it made me feel insecure...and when I feel like that I throw my weight around——'

'And smoulder with jealousy.'

Cesare tensed under the charge and finally nodded, brilliant dark eyes clinging almost pleadingly to hers.

'There was no need for that,' Mina whispered shakily. 'I never stopped loving you either.'

He looked dazed, as though that had been the very last thing he had expected to hear. 'But——'

'But what?' Mina demanded, her tumultuous emotions sweeping her with sudden violent impatience.

'Clayton...I thought——'

'I told you I loved you weeks ago and you flung it back in my face!'

'I thought you didn't mean it,' he confessed.

'You want it written in blood and framed?'

'How can you love me after everything I've done?' he breathed raggedly. 'I thought Clayton——'

'Will you please shut up about Steve?' Mina interrupted in despair. 'I never loved Steve. I didn't even fancy him. That was why we broke up.'

Cesare moved closer. 'He's a very handsome man...if you go for the local yokel type in wellies,' he could not resist extending, and she tried not to smile. 'You didn't fancy him? I thought that I had come between the two of you. That's why I asked you to marry me, why I came back the same day for your answer because I couldn't stand the suspense! Then you said yes, but only for

LYNNE GRAHAM

185

Susie,' he recalled, his English losing its clarity with
stress.

'Isn't that the same excuse you employed to propose?'

'I thought I was only getting you because I was rich.'

'Nope... you got me because I loved you.'

He closed his arms round her so tightly and so suddenly that she feared for her ribcage. 'I love you too,'
he said with fierce unsteadiness and an audible overload
of relief. 'I couldn't bear to lose you again.'

'I'm not going anywhere.' Mina framed his hard
cheekbones with her hands and stared up at him with
possessive eyes, a wild, glorious happiness flooding
through her in waves.

'You picked a bedroom three doors away...'

'Next to Susie in case she wakes up in the night... she
doesn't know this house. I'll have to leave the door ajar
and the light on out on the landing.'

'What does she do when she wakes up?'

'Climbs into bed with me. Welcome to the joys of
parenthood.' Mina's voice shook at his look of consternation. 'You have a lot to learn. Susie generally wakes
up at dawn. She bounces onto my bed and talks non-
stop. If you look like you're not listening, she gets on
top of you and tickles you.'

'We need a nanny,' Cesare decided.

'My, but you're changing your tune...'

Cesare looked down at her with hungry golden eyes
that grabbed at her heart. He kissed her with soul-
shattering tenderness and her knees gave way. He
trembled against her and held her close for long, timeless
minutes in silence. 'Te amo...te amo,' he whispered then
with raw emotion and kissed her again, sending all her
senses flying off on a sensual voyage of rediscovery.

A long while later, Mina shifted languorously in his
arms and grinned. 'I think Freddy needs a mate——'

'A what?'

'We could call her Florence, set them side by side for
company...in a dark corner somewhere,' Mina proffered.

'They might breed...' Abruptly, Cesare surged upright and stared down at her in horror.

'What's wrong?'

'I didn't take any precautions this afternoon.'

'So?' Mina was unconcerned.

'*Dio*...what happens if you're——?'

'You stay in the waiting-room,' she told him gently. 'You'd be safer there.'

'I will be with you,' he informed her loftily.

And he was, a little shaky on his feet but his nerves of steel carrying him through. Mina was very relieved when their son arrived quickly and naturally. Cesare was even more relieved. And Freddy Fish? Freddy got an entire family to keep him company in his not so dark corner...

THIS TIME, FOREVER

Four years ago Darcy made a pass at heartthrob
Keir Robards. And he turned her down flat.

BUT

NOW

HE'S

BACK!

And Darcy is determined to make him pay....

#1831 FAST AND LOOSE
by Elizabeth Oldfield

Available in August wherever
Harlequin books are sold.

HARLEQUIN PRESENTS®

TTF2

HARLEQUIN PRESENTS®

Ties of Passion
by Sally Wentworth

The story of the Brodey family. Money, looks, style—the
Brodeys have everything...except love.

Read part one of this exciting three-part series

#1832 CHRIS

Chris Brodey could offer Tiffany anything she wanted,
but she soon discovered that he wasn't a man prepared to
give something for nothing....

**Watch for books two and three in
September and October!**

Available in August wherever Harlequin books are sold.

TOPG

BRIDE'S BAY RESORT

UNLOCK THE DOOR TO GREAT ROMANCE AT BRIDE'S BAY RESORT

Join Harlequin's new across-the-lines series, set in an exclusive hotel on an island off the coast of South Carolina.

Seven of your favorite authors will bring you exciting stories about fascinating heroes and heroines discovering love at Bride's Bay Resort.

Look for these fabulous stories coming to a store near you beginning in January 1996.

Harlequin American Romance #613 in January
Matchmaking Baby by Cathy Gillen Thacker

Harlequin Presents #1794 in February
Indiscretions by Robyn Donald

Harlequin Intrigue #362 in March
Love and Lies by Dawn Stewardson

Harlequin Romance #3404 in April
Make Believe Engagement by Day Leclaire

Harlequin Temptation #588 in May
Stranger in the Night by Roseanne Williams

Harlequin Superromance #695 in June
Married to a Stranger by Connie Bennett

Harlequin Historicals #324 in July
Dulcie's Gift by Ruth Langan

Visit Bride's Bay Resort each month wherever Harlequin books are sold.

HARLEQUIN ®

BBAYG

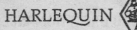

HARLEQUIN ✦ PRESENTS®

PRIVATE & CONFIDENTIAL

MEMO

To: The Reader

From: The Editor at Harlequin Presents

Subject: #1829 BEYOND ALL REASON
by Cathy Williams

Abigail knew her gorgeous boss, Ross Anderson,
couldn't seriously be attracted to her. But
should Abigail listen to reason, or follow
her heart?

P.S. Available in August wherever
Harlequin books are sold.

Look us up on-line at: http://www.romance.net

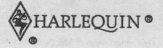